WELCOME
TO
VIETNAM

"HEY! YOU ——ING FRESH MEAT! THE CONG ARE GOING TO *KILL* YOU!" The voice came from out of the pack of soldiers standing behind the cyclone fence waiting to board the jet.

In the bus Barnett tried pushing out the heavy screen that covered the windows, but the bolts were well seated. His face turned red, and he slammed his hand against the screen and made an obscene gesture. The soldier who had shouted at the new guys dropped his bag and started climbing the fence to get at him. Barnett pressed his face against the heavy screen and yelled, "I ——ED YOUR GIRL BEFORE I LEFT THE STATES!"

The soldier fought against his friends to climb the fence and get at Barnett.

"...AND SHE'S PREGNANT!"

The bus driver started pulling away. He knew that if he waited there would be a riot...

SURVIVOR OF
NAM BAPTISM

Also by Donald E. Zlotnik

Survivor of Nam: P.O.W.
Survivor of Nam: Black Market

Forthcoming from
POPULAR LIBRARY

SURVIVOR OF
NAM · BAPTISM

DONALD E. ZLOTNIK

POPULAR LIBRARY

An Imprint of Warner Books, Inc.

A Warner Communications Company

POPULAR LIBRARY EDITION

Copyright © 1988 by Warner Books, Inc.
All rights reserved.

Cover design by Jackie Merri Meyer
Cover photograph by Burgess Blevins

Popular Library books are published by
Warner Books, Inc.
666 Fifth Avenue
New York, N.Y. 10103

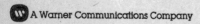 A Warner Communications Company

Printed in the United States of America

First Printing: February, 1988

10 9 8 7 6 5 4 3 2 1

Dear Mom and Dad,

I guess this will be my last letter to you from the States. They're flying us out to Saigon tomorrow by TWA. Its not a normal flight but somekinda charter thing.

Its kinda funny. You meet a lot of guys when you're in training but really can't keep in touch with them. Every body is always going off in different directions. There's this one guy who I've managed to stick with long enough to get on first name basis. His name is Spencer Barnett, and he's a good old boy (best soldier in the outfit). We're flyin out together tomorrow.

All in all basic training wasn't that bad. And you hear a lot about guys from the inner city being crooks and punks and stuff, but you know some of them are just alright guys. I guess you can't believe everything that you hear. I hope the same is true about Vietnam. . . .

David

O N E

<u>Maneater</u>

The jungle was silent; even the insects sensed that a powerful, destructive force was passing their hiding places along the narrow deer path.

At over seven hundred pounds, she was very large for a Southeast Asian tiger, and would have been a perfect trophy for any big-game hunter except for the large patch of burned hide that covered her right hip. She had been hunting six months earlier and had just made a kill when the B-52 strike hit. A large, burning piece of hardwood tree hit her with the force of a truck, breaking her hipbone in eight places. The kill she had just made saved her life as she lay near it for three weeks in severe pain. For thirty meters around, the jungle was leveled from the blows of her paws and the crunching of her large teeth as she fought the pain and slowly healed. Her hip fused together with a bizarre twenty-degree bend in it that made it impossible for her to hunt deer and wild boar. She could no longer use her rear legs to leap, nor could she sprint for the necessary charge to capture wild game.

The bomb strike had lasted less than five minutes in the

triple-canopied jungle that bordered the South Vietnamese
valley of the A Shau and had been planned because of a
reconnaissance team's sighting of a large North Vietnamese force moving across the border toward the A Shau Valley. The F-4 pilots had executed the routine mission
without reporting any ground fire or antiaircraft activity,
which almost always signaled that the enemy was long
gone from the area. A report of ground fire during the
bombing mission would have brought at least one infantry
company from the 1st Cavalry Division to sweep the area
for dead enemy soldiers and a body count for headquarters.
It was ironic because six of the five-hundred-pound bombs
had landed dead center on a sleeping NVA Sapper Company that was assigned to harass the large American bases
surrounding Da Nang to the west.

The tigress increased her pace as she drew near to the
site where the explosions had occurred the night before.
Her deformed hip joint and bones changed what would
have been normally a beautiful, graceful gait into a pathetic
hobble, but she hadn't missed a meal in six months and
knew that when the loud noises stopped, there would be
something dead to eat nearby.

The five-hundred-pound bombs had torn through the
crude overnight shelters the NVA soldiers had erected.
Most of the Sapper Company had been sleeping in their
hammocks two or three feet off the ground, and the frag-
ments from the bombs had cut through them like a chain
saw gone wild. The few survivors of the bombing were
stumbling around in shell shock when the first rays of daylight filtered through the trees.

She paused in the jungle at the edge of the bomb crater
and smelled the good odor of bloody flesh. A slight movement caught her eye near a pile of cut bamboo, and she
hobbled through the jungle around the small clearing over
to where she could have a better view. A man lay propped

up against the side of the wet, earthy-smelling hole in the ground and was trying to tie a piece of cloth around his bare waist. She crouched low and growled; live meat that couldn't run away was always better than meat that was already dead.

He looked up just in time to see the big cat hobbling across the small clearing toward him on three legs. The NVA captain reached for his pistol and almost had it out of its holster when she reached him.

The door of the TWA charter flight opened and let in the bright daylight. Private First Class David Woods remained in his seat with his seat belt still fastened as a symbolic gesture that he really didn't want to leave the airplane. He wasn't the only one. The jet was filled with soldiers being assigned to Vietnam, and the aircraft had just landed on the tarmac of the huge U.S. Army airfield at Saigon. A sergeant wearing a neat, short-sleeved khaki uniform and carrying a clipboard entered the civilian aircraft.

"Who's the group leader?" The sergeant looked down the aisle at the familiar scared faces.

"Here, Sergeant!" A tall armor captain stood up and walked down the aisle. He handed the sergeant the flight manifest, with all of the soldiers' names listed on it in alphabetical order.

"When I call out your name, leave the aircraft and board one of the buses that are parked outside. We'll be taking all of you to Camp Alpha, where you'll be in-processed and assigned to a unit." To Woods, the sergeant's voice sounded bored.

There were over two hundred men on the aircraft, and since his last name started with W, Woods knew that it would be a while before he would leave the comfort and security of the seat he had been sitting in for the past twenty-two hours. He caught quick glimpses of the men as they passed his seat, and he could see that all of them, even the officers, had large, wet sweat stains under their armpits.

"Woods . . ." The sergeant looked up from the manifest. "Woods, David!"

He heard the voice calling his name as if from out of a tunnel a million miles away and heard himself answering, "Here, Sergeant!" As he walked toward the exit, he saw that the opening was shining brightly, as if to give him direction to Vietnam and the war that was being fought on the other side. David took a deep breath and stepped through the archway. His senses registered three things almost simultaneously: the heat smashing against his face; a strong smell of jet exhaust; and a new smell, the *smell* of Vietnam.

"Shag your ass, Woods!" An arm waved to him from the front seat of the first bus in line.

Woods moved quickly toward the closing bus door and squeezed in between the rubber safety guards. He gave the Air Force driver a dirty look and then slipped down on the seat Barnett had saved for him. "Thanks, Spencer."

"Fuck it! I'd have done the same for a nigger." Barnett looked out of the window as he spoke. Cloth tape had been put around the edges of each of the bus windows and then crossed through the center. Woods guessed that the tape was put there to keep the glass from flying through the bus in case of a mortar or bomb attack on the air base. The tape was the first real sign that he was in a war zone and not another Stateside military base.

"You should ease up on the name-calling, Spencer. We're all in the same boat over here."

"It ain't no different here or back in the States—a nigger is a nigger—except here you have to watch your back more often!" Spencer Barnett kept looking out of the window at the long rows of soldiers waiting under an open-air tin-roofed building for the TWA jet to refuel so that they could load up for the trip back to the States.

Woods looked around his seat and saw that most of the blacks were sitting together near the back of the bus and out of hearing distance. "Those guys must be going home." David pointed at the group under the tin roof.

"Yeah!" Barnett grinned. "When I go back, I'm going to have so fucking many ribbons on my chest, you're going to have to stand next to me to help hold them!"

"You're fucking crazy, Spencer!" Woods grinned and felt good that Barnett hadn't changed on him. Barnett had gone through basic training and advanced infantry training with him and had been the source of constant trouble and entertainment for the whole company. Spencer Barnett came from a small South Carolina town, and he hated blacks, especially Northern blacks, with a passion. He had ended up having to fight every single black soldier in his basic company, and most of the blacks when he went through advanced training. He had won about half of the fights and had fought to a draw in another third of the one-on-one battles. Barnett was so hopelessly prejudiced that the drill sergeants had given up on him and ignored most of his snide remarks. If it hadn't been for the Vietnam War, Barnett surely would have been discharged from the service, but even the most bitter black drill sergeant saw the fighting man in Barnett and knew that he would be put to good use in Vietnam.

"Hey! You fucking fresh meat! The Cong are going to kill you!" The voice came from out of the pack of soldiers standing behind the cyclone fence waiting to board the jet.

Barnett tried pushing out the heavy screen that covered the windows on the bus, but the bolts were well-seated. The screens had been placed over each of the windows to prevent a Sapper's hand grenade or satchel charge from coming into the troop carrier. Barnett's face turned red, and he slammed his hand against the screen and made an obscene gesture with his middle finger. The soldier dropped his duffel bag and started climbing the fence to get at the man in the bus. Barnett pressed his face against the heavy screen and yelled, *"I fucked your girl before I left the States!"*

The soldier fought against his friends to climb the fence and get at Barnett.

"And she's pregnant!"

The bus driver started pulling away from the close proximity of the departing soldiers, knowing that if he waited there for the rest of the buses to load up, a riot would start between the two groups.

Barnett dropped back in his seat fuming; he wanted a fight so he could burn off some of the tension that was boiling inside of him.

The doors opened, and the sergeant who had boarded the jet earlier hopped up the steps and nodded for the driver to depart. The ride over to Camp Alpha was short, a half-mile of the trip along the perimeter of the huge base. The sergeant looked back at the rows of young faces; all of them were looking out of the windows in the same direction, at the fighting bunkers and the rows of wooden shacks that started where the barbed wire stopped. The sergeant harbored the same thought he always had when he picked up the new arrivals: How many of them would return to the States in one piece and alive?

A gate guard stopped the bus and made a cursory check of the undercarriage, knowing that the vehicle had not left the air base but following his written directions. He nodded at the sergeant, and the bus moved slowly forward through the wood-and-barbed-wire gate.

PFC Woods stared out of his window at the plywood-and-tin barracks lining both sides of the asphalt road. He had heard about the hootches and had seen them on the evening news. The buildings seemed small now that he was close to them. The construction was very simple; a wooden frame and a plywood floor with sheets of plywood tacked around the structure four feet up, and the rest of the space covered by fine screening to keep out some of the mosquitoes.

The sergeant ordered the men to fall into two ranks and let them smoke until the trucks carrying their baggage arrived from the airport. Woods and Barnett found their gear and carried their duffel bags into the nearest empty hootch.

Barnett looked around the open squad bay and saw that there was a door leading out of the back. He set his bags down, walked over to the screen door, and pushed it open to look outside. A latrine and a shower were right outside their building. "Fuck this shit, Woods!" Barnett turned to face his friend. "I don't want to have to spend the night smelling shit!" Barnett picked up his gear and exited through the back door. "Come on! We'll find a place near the perimeter."

Woods hesitated and then lifted his heavy duffel bag off the floor. Right now, he would rather have Barnett as a friend than an enemy. "Don't you think the sergeant will get pissed if we leave?"

"What the fuck is he going to do to us? Send us to Vietnam?" Barnett chuckled at his own joke. He stopped walking when he reached the last barracks in the long line of buildings and entered this time through the back door. The building was empty. "Pick a bed!" Barnett dropped his gear on the cot nearest to the rear door, and Woods selected the bed across from him. Both soldiers could hear the sergeant calling for the men to fall out for chow. Three more soldiers rushed into the hootch and dropped their bags on the beds near the front door before rushing back outside.

Night was beginning to fall as the new replacements stood in the long line outside of the mess-hall building.

Woods watched the Camp Alpha cadre enter and exit the building through the cadre exit. He noticed that all of them were relaxed and none of them carried any weapons. The line moved slowly. Barnett lit up a Kool cigarette and inhaled the smoke deep into his lungs. Woods noticed that his basic training buddy was very nervous; Barnett always hot-boxed his cigarettes when he was nervous. When they were waiting for it to get dark in basic so that they could crawl the night infiltration course, Barnett had hot-boxed his smokes.

"War getting to you?" David said, trying to start a conversation with Barnett.

A look of pure hate flashed in Barnett's eyes. "*Nothing* gets to me! *Nothing!*"

"Just asking, Spencer . . . just asking!"

"Fuck this shit!" Barnett left the chow line. "I'm not going to wait all night for some shit food!"

Woods nodded and watched his hyper bunkmate stride off toward the perimeter.

The food was bland but edible, for replacement-center food. David made a thick sandwich before he left the building and stepped out into the night. He didn't realize that it could get dark so fast. Lights were blinking on and off behind draped doors and window flaps, giving off enough light to see by on his way back to his hootch. He was stopped by another one of the replacements, whom he recognized from the airplane, and was asked directions back to their hootches. The man had failed to orient himself before entering the mess hall.

Woods found his hootch and walked down the dark aisle between the bunks until he found his duffel bag. He saw that Barnett wasn't on his cot and went to the back door and peered out.

"You back already?" The voice came from a sandbag bunker twenty feet behind the hootch.

"Yeah, I brought you a sandwich."

"What kind?"

"Pork chop." David handed Barnett the sandwich.

"Smells good. Maybe I should have eaten." Barnett unwrapped the thick sandwich and took a bite. "Fuck!"

"What's wrong?"

"The bones are still in there!"

"Oh, yeah . . . forgot about that."

Barnett started laughing, and Woods joined him. It was funny how sometimes a small thing could cut right through the tension.

"Hop up and have a seat . . . it's the best view in town!" Barnett patted the sandbags with his free hand.

"Might as well. There's nothing else going on tonight in this shithole place." Woods took a seat on the sandbag personnel bunker that was used only as overhead protection in case of a rocket or mortar attack. A series of mortar pops echoed back to the two men from the perimeter, followed shortly by four flares lighting up the night sky. An M-60 light machine gun broke through the quasi-silence of the base. Woods watched the red tracers arch over the flat terrain and bounce off the ground before losing their light. It was a pretty sight in a macabre sort of way.

"I don't think I remember where you said you were from." Barnett adjusted the sandbag he was sitting on. "Michigan?"

"Naw, I'm from Lincoln, Nebraska . . . the state capital."

"No shit!" Barnett exaggerated the words, trying to be sarcastic.

Woods stacked up a small pile of the sandbags from the roof of the bunker and made a backrest out of them. He leaned back and crossed his legs. It was a couple of minutes before he spoke again to Barnett. "Why do you try so damn hard to make people hate you?"

Barnett threw the pork-chop bones into the dark, as far

away as he could from the bunker. He scooted over to the edge of the sandbag covered roof and dropped down to the ground, leaving Woods alone without answering his question.

The perimeter guards popped hand flares and fired an occasional round at suspicious shadows. Woods noticed that there were sections of the perimeter where the Vietnamese civilians had built their shacks so close that some of the small buildings actually touched the barbed wire. David thought that if he were a Vietcong, he would use the shacks as a cover to get close to the base before exposing himself. Soft footsteps coming from behind him caused Woods to lean over on his side and look around. Barnett had returned carrying two of the blankets from the hootch cots.

"It's getting a little cold out here." Barnett threw one of the blankets to Woods.

"You're right. I didn't think it would get chilly in Vietnam, but when the sun goes down, the temperature must drop fifteen degrees."

"I wonder when we're going to get our weapons." Barnett wrapped the blanket around his shoulders and sat Indian-style on the bunker next to Woods.

"I was thinking the same thing. I sure wouldn't want to be caught in an attack without a weapon."

Barnett's next comment caught David off-guard. He thought that Barnett had left the bunker because he didn't want to talk about himself. "Do you think that I *try* to make people hate me?"

"You sure make it seem that way. I mean, look at the way you talk about blacks." Woods pulled the blanket together near his throat and shivered. "Spencer, you fought just about every black in basic and AIT . . . even the drill instructors wanted to kick your ass. In fact, I heard that they were planning an NCO blanket party for you in the showers one night and you lucked out and drew guard duty.

Yeah, it seems like you go out of your way to make people hate you."

"*Fuck* people." Barnett's words carried a force that precluded the need for an exclamation mark.

David sat quietly in the dark on the bunker with Barnett; neither of them spoke for a long while. Woods wasn't taken in by Barnett's exterior hatred; he had seen too many acts of kindness from the man that had always been covered over by gruff talk and hostile acts. He remembered one time in basic when they were on their qualifying twenty-mile hike and one of their classmates twisted his ankle and couldn't carry his pack and march at the same time. Barnett took the man's pack and carried it the remainder of the hike, but only after he called the man a wimp and a pussy. The point was, though, that he had carried the other man's heavy pack in addition to his own when no one else would.

"You *rich*?" Barnett spit out the word.

"No, we're sort of middle-class. My dad's an insurance broker and my mother works. . . ."

"Where?"

"She's a secretary at the post office." David's voice mellowed, and good thoughts of home filled his mind. "She decided to work so that she could pay for my brother and me to go to college on a first-class ticket. My brother's in med school now."

"Why didn't you go to college?"

"I went for part of my freshman year, but . . ." Woods adjusted himself on the sandbags that still retained most of the heat from the day. "I don't know . . . there was a big antiwar movement at Lincoln Community College, and I didn't think that it was right. . . ."

"What was right?"

"For me to be protected because we had enough money to send me to college, and guys whose parents weren't rich enough to hide their kids in colleges had to watch them go to war and at the same time put up with all of the protesting from the college kids who were protected from serving. It just didn't seem right."

"So you decided on doing your part...a middle-class hero!" Barnett tried chuckling but failed. It took a lot of guts for Woods to drop out of college to serve in the Army and take all of the harassment from his friends and family.

"And you? Why did you join the United States Army *Infantry*, asshole?"

"I didn't have much of a choice. Fucking *jail* or the Army. The judge gave me those two options." Barnett chuckled. "He even told me that I would have a chance to kill people if I hurried up and joined before the war was over!"

"It sounds like the judge you had was a nice guy!"

"Fuck them! They were all *nice* guys." Barnett talked as he made himself a sandbag backrest like David's. "I spent most of my life in foster homes and the juvenile center. Have you ever been to a juve in South Carolina?"

"No, I can't say that I have."

"They're ninety-nine percent niggers!" Barnett spit out a stream of tobacco. "I was a little shit then, and they kicked my ass every fucking day...but I fought back! Them fuckers would pound my ass until I couldn't stand up, and I'd reach out and trip one of them when they were leaving! I fought back!"

Woods was beginning to understand what motivated Barnett to fight blacks.

"Niggers yell prejudice, especially niggers from the North, but you ain't seen prejudice until you've been the only white kid in a juve filled with blacks! I hate them motherfuckers!"

"Didn't the staff stop them from beating up on you?" Woods lit up a Salem.

"The fucking *staff* was mostly niggers. You know, *equal-opportunity* shit!"

"Well, if most of the kids in the juve were black, it would make sense that the staff should be black."

Woods couldn't see the glare coming from Barnett in the dark. "Then they should have a juve for whites only!"

"That's segregation, Spencer."

"So fucking what!"

Woods realized that he wasn't going to make any progress with Barnett on the topic of race and changed the subject slightly. "What about your foster home?"

"What about it?"

"Didn't you like it there?"

A long pause filled the next ten minutes before Barnett answered. "Yeah, I liked it there . . . I *loved* it there."

"So why did you leave?"

"The social worker thought that I was becoming *too* close to my foster family, and she was supposed to work things out so that I would go back to my mother and step-asshole!" Barnett lit up a cigarette along with his chew. "She had me pulled from the foster home. It was a farm . . . I loved it there, man! I was *free* and could fish. We would go hunting for rabbits and coon. My dad—you know, my *foster* dad—and his son and I . . . I loved it there so damn much! That fucking bitch!"

A hand flare popped above the distant bunker line, and Woods could see the tears running down Barnett's cheeks.

"I ain't *never* going to let people hurt me like that again . . . *never!*" Barnett took a long pull from his cigarette. "I showed her ass a thing or two! I fucked her up, and two of her wimpy-assed queer social-worker friends!"

"You fucked her up?"

"When they took me from my foster home and were holding me at the social services center until I could be taken to the new foster home, I punched the bitch in the mouth! Two of her coworkers tried holding me down on the floor, and I kneed one of them in the nuts and bit the other cocksucker on his chest. I mean, I *bit* that dicksucker and spit out the piece of skin on the floor!"

David swallowed so that he wouldn't throw up. "How old were you then?"

"Twelve." Barnett's voice had lowered considerably. "That's when they decided to throw my ass in the juve."

"Hey, you guys mind if we join you up there?" The voice came from the bottom of the bunker.

"Sure, we don't give a fuck . . . it's government property." Barnett wiped his face with the back of his hand.

"Thanks." Three new replacements climbed up to the top of the bunker. The same one spoke again. "We couldn't sleep. I guess it's the time change."

One of the quiet ones rolled and lit up a joint. "Want some blow?"

"Naw, I don't do that shit!" Barnett answered for himself and Woods.

"You guys are going to have it tough over here if you don't do dope. They say the time goes by faster if you use blow." The same skinny soldier spoke to Barnett.

"I came over here to *kill* fucking gooks. If I wanted to smoke that shit, I would have gone to California!" Barnett's tone of voice was enough warning to the trio, and they quietly moved over to the far side of the bunker to smoke.

"Well I don't give a fuck what they say about you, Barnett . . . I like your raunchy Southern ass." Woods pulled his blanket tightly around his shoulders and scooted down so that he could use his backrest as a pillow. "I think I'll spend the rest of the night out here."

Barnett didn't answer Woods but rolled over onto his side and feigned sleep. He hated making friends because he feared being hurt again, and that was something he had sworn would never happen again. He had loved his foster family unconditionally, and they hadn't even tried seeing him in the five years he had spent in the South Carolina juvenile system. What Spencer Barnett didn't know was that his foster father had spent thirty days in jail for contempt of court when he swore at the female social worker in front of the judge and her two male coworkers. Spencer Barnett had been put on the social welfare system's mosthated list by the three representatives of the State of South Carolina, and for five years they had plotted behind the boy's back, even to the extent of insuring that when the judge allowed for his release at seventeen years old to join the Army, he was shipped out so that his foster father was prevented from knowing what had happened to the teenager.

The replacement-center barracks sergeant took roll call again to make sure that the five missing men hadn't joined the predawn formation while he had been talking to the company commander. The same five names brought no response from the formation.

"Where in the hell could they have gone?" The senior company sergeant rubbed his chin. It was the first time since he had been assigned to the replacement depot that soldiers had gone AWOL.

"Are you asking me?" The barracks sergeant tapped his clipboard with his pen. "How the fuck would I know?"

"Sergeant?" One of the replacements stepped forward from his position in the first rank. "I remember seeing three guys heading back to the perimeter bunkers right after we ate. It was just getting dark out."

"Back toward the perimeter?" The whole statement was a question. "What in the fuck were they going back there for?"

The soldier shrugged his shoulders like he didn't know

the answer; helping find missing guys was one thing, but ratting on people would get his ass kicked. "You got me, Sergeant."

"Go back there and check the personnel bunkers for them." The senior sergeant nodded at his NCO.

The barracks sergeant cursed under his breath and left the formation. Streaks of light were breaking over the top of the buildings to the east, giving off enough light to see by and making the flashlight he carried ineffective.

Woods heard the sergeant approaching the bunker and raised his head off the sandbag pillow. Barnett was also awake and sat up.

"Well! So you fucking heads decided on having a first-night party!" The sergeant slapped his clipboard against the side of the sandbag bunker and reached up with his free hand to remove the hash pipe from where the three replacements had left it. "God damn you! Now get your asses moving!"

"He thinks we did dope," David whispered to Barnett.

"Shut up." Barnett hopped down from the bunker. "Sorry about being late, Sergeant. We didn't know the formation would be so early."

"We'll see how you motherfuckers like smelling *shit*!" The sergeant shook one of the soldiers who was still sleeping. "You like smoking this shit, huh, boy?" The man woke up in a haze.

"Yes, Sergeant!" He hadn't realized what he was saying.

"Oh, you're a smartass too!" The sergeant pulled him off the bunker. Woods noticed that two of the men who had joined them the night before were black, and the third man, the one the sergeant pulled off the bunker, was white. "Well, I'll let you all smell what burning shit is really like! All of you are on the shit-burning detail this morning!"

Barnett shrugged his shoulders. He didn't know what the

sergeant was talking about, and neither did the rest of the replacements.

The barracks sergeant had marched the five of them to the mess hall for breakfast and then back to the barracks, where he showed them the seven latrines. Sewage pipes didn't exist in the large American bases, and the engineers had designed latrines like the old outhouses from the American past, with a few modernizations. The old-fashioned pit or hole under the outhouse seat had been replaced by half of a fifty-five-gallon drum with large steel handles welded on it. The barracks latrines had eight seats with two-foot-high partitions nailed between each seat so that a soldier could wipe his ass with a little privacy. Those were the better-built ones; the latrines for enlisted men usually didn't have the seat dividers. The idea behind the fifty-five-gallon drums to collect the feces and urine was to be able to burn the feces rather than having to dig new holes and move the latrines. The idea was a good one and reduced the chance of flies feeding on the latrine by-products for lunch and then having their supper in the mess halls.

"I can't believe this shit!" The white soldier from the trio of heads held the long steel rod with the hooked end in his hands. The back flap of the latrine was up, and eight full tubs of feces waited to be pulled out in the clearing and set on fire with diesel fuel. "That fucking sergeant wants me to drag that shit out here?"

"Move your ass, motherfucker! You're the fucking reason Woods and I are out here!" Barnett said, ready to fight.

David looked over at the two blacks who were already setting the first four half-barrels on fire. They glanced up at Barnett but didn't interfere; they knew he was right and was being punished for something he hadn't done.

Barnett looked at the skinny white soldier with disgust, walked over to the back of the latrine, and pulled the barrel out with his bare hand. He removed the remaining three barrels, and Woods poured diesel fuel over the piles of feces before igniting them.

"Man! Shit even stinks when it burns!" Barnett put his hands on his hips and watched the thick black pillars of smoke rise straight up in the breezeless sky.

Woods stood next to Barnett and watched, smelling the odor that would never leave his senses as long as he lived.

"Come on, we've got a bunch more to do!" Barnett had become the natural leader of the shit-burning detail.

The sun was hot when they reached the last latrine, and all of them were in a hurry to get finished and back to their barracks. The unit assignments were due to be posted on the company bulletin board.

"Look at this motherfuckin' shit!" Kirkpatrick, one of the blacks who had been smoking hash the night before, spoke for the first time to the group. One of the latrine seats was missing a tub, and a large pile of feces and toilet paper was under the wooden hole.

"Now I know why the sergeant gave us the shovel." Woods had been carrying the long-handled shovel from latrine to latrine.

"You guys pull out the tubs, and Woods can spread that shit out in each of them that aren't too full." Barnett braced the wooden flap up, and the remainder of the detail started pulling out the half-barrels.

"Hot motherfucker!" Kirkpatrick's buddy spoke to the group for the first time. Brown's high-pitched voice operated that high for a reason. A seven-foot-long snake slithered out from between two of the barrels and stopped when its stomach touched the hot sand. "What kind of motherfucking snake is that?"

Woods swung the shovel in an arch, cutting the snake's head off five inches below the hood. "Cobra. A king cobra if I'm not mistaken. . . ."

"In a shitter!" The skinny white soldier reached for his balls; he was thinking about the shit he had taken during the night in the latrine near the bunker.

"Probably was looking for rats." Woods struck again with the shovel at the twisting mass of black coils.

"What have you guys found?" The barracks sergeant had joined the detail during the execution of the cobra.

"Snake." Barnett spoke the word like the reptile had been one of his friends.

"What kind?"

"Cobra."

"Bullshit! Man, there aren't any cobras around here!" The sergeant stepped toward the chopped-up snake.

"Pick up its head and see," Barnett said, challenging the NCO.

"Fuck me! It *is* a cobra!" The sergeant took a step backward. "Where was it hiding?"

"In the shitter," Woods enjoyed telling the sergeant. He could imagine the NCO inspecting the shitter every time he went to the john.

"I'd better let the first sergeant know about this." He turned to Woods with the shovel. "Bring the snake with you over to the orderly room."

"What do you want us to do?" Barnett said to the NCO.

"Go wash up and report to the supply sergeant. Woods will join you after he shows the first sergeant that damn snake!"

Barnett sat on a pile of dirty blankets and clothes in the supply tent. He had already counted the items and listed them on the forms. Woods had gone to check the company bulletin board for their assignments. The barracks sergeant had taken the five-man detail over to the finance office and had the detail cut ahead of the line to exchange their American money for military payment certificates. Barnett was

looking at the small paper bills that represented coins in the
United States. It seemed funny having paper represent a
quarter.

"Get used to that shit! You won't see real money for a
year unless you go on R and R." One of the supply sergeants spoke to Barnett.

"Do the Vietnamese downtown take this stuff?"

"You had better bet your ass they do!" The young sergeant laughed. "The whores know when they're going to
change MPC before we do!"

"What do you mean?" Barnett folded his money and
shoved it back in his pocket.

"Every six months or so we have to turn in all of our
MPC money, and they issue us new stuff. The idea is to
stop us from screwing up the local economy and to stop
black marketing." The sergeant shook his head. "It only
ends up hassling the fucking field troops, who usually are
the ones who get fucked."

"I don't plan on having enough cash to get fucked!"
Barnett had set up an allotment so that most of his money
went into a military savings program that yielded ten percent interest.

"You do want to keep enough to get *fucked* . . .
downtown, that is." The sergeant looked up at Woods entering through the tent door. "Good, you're back. Let's
load this stuff up and haul it downtown to the civilian
laundry."

Barnett looked at Woods, who shook his head; their assignments hadn't been posted yet. "Some of the guys have
already left, but we're not under shipping orders."

"Don't rush it, guys!" The sergeant was serious. "Every
day you spend here is being counted as one day in Vietnam. Don't rush it!"

Woods and Barnett sat at the tailgate of the truck, and
the three heads sat up near the cab of the truck where the

wind wasn't so bad and they could share a pipe. The young supply sergeant was the one who had provided the blow.

Woods was engrossed in the people lining the streets of the large Vietnamese capital city. The *cao-dai* dresses the women wore were interesting, but every time Woods saw a man wearing a pair of black pants and shirt, he thought of the Vietcong. They still hadn't been issued weapons, and Woods felt nervous riding in the back of an open truck.

Barnett thought out loud. "I want a fucking gun!" He had been thinking along the same lines as Woods.

The truck stopped in front of a large warehouse building, backed up to a set of double doors that opened, and three Vietnamese men jumped down into the truck and started unloading the bundles.

The young supply sergeant walked around to the rear of the idling deuce-and-a-half and spoke up to the detail. "If any of you want to hit a steam bath before we leave, there's a good one over there." He pointed to a bamboo-fronted lean-to-style building down the street.

"Who in the fuck needs a steam bath in this fucking heat!" Kirkpatrick said from the front of the truck.

"You can get your ashes hauled too."

"Oh, yeah!" Brown, Kirkpatrick's buddy, was interested. "How much?"

"Five dollars for a steam bath and head . . . five extra if you want to fuck." The sergeant looked at his watch. "I'll wait an hour for you."

Brown jumped over the railing, followed by the skinny white soldier and Kirkpatrick.

"Are you two going?" the sergeant said to Barnett.

"Yeah . . . why the fuck not!" Barnett hopped over the tailgate and looked back at Woods, who shrugged his shoulders and joined him.

The Vietnamese madam smiled, revealing a betel-nut-stained set of teeth.

"I wouldn't let her suck me off using *your* cock!" Barnett whispered to Woods.

"There should be some better ones inside." Woods hoped his words were true, and they were. A group of giggling, young girls in their late teens or early twenties greeted the five soldiers and showed them where they could undress. A pile of towels was stacked on a low bench. Brown had half an erection when he undressed and wrapped his towel around his waist quickly before the others could see. The steam room was small and barely held the five men. Woods stayed only for a few minutes and stepped out of the makeshift enclosure. He heard someone moan from behind a drawn curtain and guessed that some other GI was exercising his equipment.

The girl pointed at the pallet, and Woods guessed that she wanted him to lie down on it. He stretched out on his stomach, and she began a rapid back massage that felt extremely good; she knew her business. David could feel his love muscle fighting to break free of the towel. She saw the slight upward shift of his hips and knew exactly what was going on under the towel. She was paid by the customer and didn't waste any time. A gentle hand tugged at David's shoulder, coaxing him to roll over on his back. He hesitated for only a second and obeyed. She hooked her finger on the top of the towel and pulled it open. David's pride sprang free. She began to give him head in a steady, deep-throated rhythm. He had had his share of sex in school, especially college, and a couple of his more loose dates had given him head before, but it was always done with a timid touch, not like this. He was proud of the size of his equipment and couldn't believe the girl was taking him in all the way to the base of his penis. He lasted less than thirty seconds but convinced himself that he had gone for a couple of minutes. The climax he experienced was total. She stroked him a couple of times and used the towel to clean him up.

"Thanks." Woods hopped down from the pallet and went back to his clothes. Barnett was already half dressed.

"That's pretty good stuff." Woods threw the towel in the basket and slipped on his pants. Barnett didn't answer.

"Oh! Yesss . . . one more time, sweet lady!" The voice came from behind a far curtain, but both Woods and Barnett could recognize Kirkpatrick's New York accent.

"I'm holding on!" Brown answered from behind a nearby curtain. "*Holding on*!"

Woods and Barnett returned to the truck before the three heads had left their booths.

"Maybe dope does make sex better. . . ." Woods said to Barnett as they lit up cigarettes.

"I'll *never* know!" Barnett flexed his jaws. "I haven't done that shit before coming here, and I ain't going to start now!"

Woods tried changing the subject. "Man, I didn't last very long in there. That was the best head I've ever gotten!" He looked over at Barnett. "How about you?"

"It was all right."

"Man, I didn't last two minutes." Woods inhaled deeply from his Kool cigarette.

"I hate fucking gooks." Barnett hissed the words out.

"Ease off, buddy." David sensed a really deep hatred.

"She was sucking my cock, but I couldn't come. That's all I thought about—how could I make love to a gook!" Barnett wouldn't look at Woods and stared down the road.

"Hey, man, that's what we're here for. You may be the only one around here with the right idea." Woods looked closely at Barnett and saw that he was an extremely handsome young man. He hadn't noticed that before, but Barnett was well built and had a pair of sparkling, dark blue eyes with thick blond hair that was cut short but still looked good on him. There was no reason why Barnett should have problems with women. Maybe it was just gooks and blacks; some people were like that. "Let's get the sergeant and get back to check the bulletin board."

"You don't think I'm fucking weird?" Barnett's voice revealed his fear.

"Like what?"

"Queer?"

"Hell, no!" Woods threw an arm over Barnett's shoulder and felt the man's muscles tighten. "I'll tell you the truth ... I didn't last two minutes ... more like thirty seconds! You don't think I have a premature ejaculation problem, do you?"

Barnett glared at Woods and then started laughing.

Kirkpatrick and Brown entertained the rest of the detail on the ride back to the replacement center with a verbal battle on who was the best lover in Vietnam. Barnett stood with his back to the group, looking out over the cab of the truck. He watched the Vietnamese pass and tried picking out which ones were Vietcong.

"I was the last one to leave the steam bath." Kirkpatrick's Brooklyn accent was high-pitched. "That's 'cuz I have *dick control*!"

"Dick control! Puerto Ricans don't have any dick control!" Brown was jive-talking his friend. "If you weren't half black, you wouldn't even know what to do with that thing of yours!"

"Before you get too carried away and everyone in New York knows you Harlem types don't know shit about women, you had better come to this long-dicked *Puerto Rican* for some lessons!" Kirkpatrick slapped his leg and then pointed at Brown.

Woods broke up the bullshit conversation. "I wonder if our orders will be posted when we get back?"

The skinny white soldier rubbed his crotch before speaking. "I don't give a fuck if they ever post any orders for me. I can handle staying here for my whole tour; there's plenty of good blow and women."

"What's your MOS?" Woods changed sides on the bed of the truck because the diesel fumes were blowing back along the right side from the exhaust stacks.

"One-one-bravo."

"Thats basic infantry. You don't have much of a chance staying here." Woods looked over at Barnett, who was ignoring all of them.

"What about you guys?" Woods addressed the other two men in the truck.

"We're both infantry." Brown spoke for both of them.

"That makes all of us infantrymen."

"Not me . . . I'm going to get the fuck out of that shit." The skinny white spoke as if he knew something the rest of them didn't.

"How you gonna do that shit?" Brown smiled. "You got a congressman pulling for you?"

"Nope. I've got two years of college, and as soon as I get to my unit, I'm going to volunteer to be a clerk."

Woods shook his head. "Good luck!"

The barracks sergeant was waiting when the laundry truck pulled up to the supply tent. Woods could see the worried look on his face, as if he had fucked up in the big time and was afraid the detail wasn't coming back. "Hurry up and get off that truck!" He ran around to the back of the vehicle. "You're shipping out in an hour!"

Barnett looked at Woods and then over at the sergeant. "Where?"

"The 1st Cavalry Division has been in a big fight up in

the Ia Drang Valley, and all the infantry MOS's in Camp Alpha are being shipped to the Cav as replacements."

All five of the replacements could hear the fear in the sergeant's voice.

"The Cav's having a lot of action?" the skinny soldier asked.

"There's rumors that the Cav has taken over five hundred casualties . . . so far." The fear was still in the sergeant's voice. The five replacements didn't know the reason why, but the sergeant was an infantryman who had pulled some strings to stay at the replacement detachment instead of joining an infantry company in the field. He was scared that if things got too bad, he would be put out in the field with five months left to do in-country.

"Hot shit!" Barnett jumped down from the truck. "Give me a gun!"

The barracks sergeant's upper lip quivered. "You're fucking crazy!" It sounded almost like he was going to break down and cry. "*Crazy!*"

T W O

Recondo

"Brown!"

"Here, Sergeant."

"Kirkpatrick!"

"Yo!"

"Woods!"

"Here, Sergeant."

"Masters!"

The skinny white soldier stopped biting his lip and answered the sergeant. "Here!"

"Barnett!"

"Here." The tone of voice was so threatening that the sergeant automatically looked up from the typed manifest for the owner. Barnett grinned.

"All right! You five have been assigned to the 3rd Brigade of the 1st Cavalry Division. They're located in Qui Nhon, on the coast up north. You'll be leaving here within an hour!" The sergeant looked back down at his clipboard and flipped through some of the papers he had attached to it. "That is, unless any of you want to volunteer for the MACV Recondo School."

"What's that?" Barnett asked.

"A three-week course in reconnaissance and commando tactics. The 3rd Brigade needs some . . . ah . . . *replacements* for their long-range recon teams." The sergeant looked up at Barnett over the edge of his clipboard. "It's good duty, and you get the best chow and equipment in the division!"

"Is it dangerous?" Brown was playing the odds; he knew that the division was engaged in a big battle and was taking a lot of casualties. Three weeks was a long time in Vietnam, and the battle would be over before they graduated from their training.

"*Everything* in Vietnam is dangerous." The sergeant tried to sound casual, but he was talking to a streetwise New Yorker who could see through a con job instantly or sooner.

"Kirkpatrick and I will go." Brown didn't give his buddy a chance to answer.

"Good!" He used a red Magic Marker to highlight their names.

"Put me down." Barnett wanted to go recon for a different reason. He looked over at Woods and questioned him with his eyes.

David shrugged his shoulders. He liked traveling in the woods back home alone and didn't think it would be much different in the jungle. A small group would be better than a large one. "Me too. Woods."

The sergeant looked over at the remaining soldier. "How about you, Masters?"

"Naw, I want to be a company clerk."

The sergeant looked at him as if he was suffering from some kind of mental illness. "A company clerk? Hey, fella, you've got a one-one-bravo MOS."

"Yeah, but I've got two years of college."

"That's great! You'll be humping a machine gun . . . you know, *complex* machinery."

"How long's the course?"

"Three weeks."

"Fuck . . . I'll go." Masters didn't like the idea very much, but it was better than going green into a major fight.

The sergeant marked the last name and grinned. "Five out of five *volunteers* for Recondo School!" He looked up from his clipboard, a sarcastic smile covering the whole bottom of his face. "You all haven't volunteered because your brigade is fighting for its ass out in the Ia Drang Valley, have you?"

"I don't see *your* ass out there!" Barnett glared at the sergeant. "Nor do I see *your* ass wearing a Recondo patch!"

"You smartass punk! I've been in Vietnam almost eleven months!" The sergeant's face was turning red.

"Doing what? Fucking with replacements?" Barnett wasn't about to back off.

"One more remark from you and you've got yourself an Article Fifteen!" The sergeant's right leg began shaking.

Barnett tightened his lips and nodded his head slightly up and down. He knew that he had hit a nerve in the sergeant.

The sergeant was the first one to look away. "Pick up your gear and follow me!" He led them to a helipad and pointed to a spot next to the perforated steel planking that was interlocked to make up a hundred-square-foot pad. Barnett was the first one to drop his duffel bag and take a seat on it to wait for their ride. The others followed suit in taking up seats in the hot sun. The sergeant left them and walked over to a shady spot next to one of the tin-roofed buildings to wait.

Two hours had passed, and Barnett was the only one still sitting in the sun; the rest of the men had found places to sit on the shady side of the building with the sergeant. Barnett glared at the NCO for most of the two hours and knew that he was getting to the other man. Sweat rolled down Barnett's chest and accumulated around the top of his pants, saturating the top three inches of his jungle fatigues.

Woods got up from his seat in the shade and went over to where the sergeant was sitting. "Is there anywhere near here where we can buy some sodas?"

The sergeant paused and then gave in. "Yeah, about a dozen tents down that road is a battalion store that sells sodas and snacks. Here, get me a Coke." He handed David a dollar. "Buy yourself one."

"You guys coming?" Woods spoke to the others leaning against the wall. He didn't even try asking Barnett.

"Yeah." Masters got up off the ground where he had been sitting. He looked back at the sergeant. "How much time do we have?"

"The chopper should have been here an hour ago." The sergeant pointed to the north. "Keep your eyes open for it, and get your asses back here quick if you see it landing!"

Woods was the first one in the battalion tent that functioned as a unit exchange. A couple of tables had been set up near the rolled-up sides, and a plywood bar occupied the rear of the structure. Pallets that had brought in artillery ammunition covered the floor. He went over to the soldier who was acting as the bartender and ordered four Shasta orange sodas. A hand-painted sign behind the bar read: NO BEER SERVED UNTIL 5 P.M.! The bartender had an open beer in his hand when Woods ordered. "Throw in a Coke, too, and a couple cans of those potato chips." He pointed to a stack of canned chips.

Masters leaned against the bar. "Do you have any blow?" He was trying to be sarcastic.

The bartender lifted the cover of a cigar box near his

elbow and removed a clear plastic pill tube of marijuana. "Two bucks." The bartender grinned at the new recruits.

"I'll be a motherfucker!" Masters was only fucking with the man. He fumbled in his pocket for the money.

Woods was already walking back to the helipad when Masters caught up to him. "Look at this shit! This is a good idea, putting blow in a plastic pill tube. It keeps it dry." He unscrewed the white cap and scraped his finger gently over the top. "It's even packed down!" He couldn't believe the buy he'd gotten on the grass. Stateside, that much blow would have cost him an easy twenty dollars.

Barnett was still staring at the sergeant when Woods returned with the cold soda. He gave the sergeant his Coke and then carried two of the Shasta orange sodas over to Spencer, along with a can of potato chips. Barnett nodded his thanks to Woods and set the sodas down on the PSP (Perforated Steel Plate) planking in the hot sun. He continued staring at the sergeant, who had opened his Coke and had most of it already gone.

"Is he fucking crazy?" the sergeant asked Woods when he returned to the shade.

"Who?" Woods played dumb.

"Barnett!"

"Naw." Woods popped open one of his Shasta orange sodas and drained the whole can in one long swallow before opening the top of his potato-chip can.

The sound of a chopper brought Kirkpatrick and Brown running to the helipad. Woods saw Brown shove a wad of MPC ten-dollar bills into his front pocket just as he reached his duffel bag.

The helicopter flight from the 1st Cavalry Division's base camp at An Khe to the Special Forces–run Recondo School at Nha Trang on the coast of the South China Sea was a pleasant flight that lasted a little longer than an hour. Woods was sitting next to Brown and Kirkpatrick, and could hear them trying to talk to each other about selling a bundle of the poncho liners back at the laundry in Saigon to the Vietnamese who ran the operation. Kirkpatrick was worried that the supply sergeant would find out about the shortage and have them court-martialed. Woods smiled to himself; now he knew where Brown had gotten the wad of money that he had seen earlier.

A Special Forces master sergeant was waiting for them at the Recondo School helipad. Instantly Barnett started sizing the NCO up. Green Berets were already becoming legendary in the Vietnam War for their exploits in long-range reconnaissance patrols.

The sergeant waited until the helicopter had departed before attempting to speak. "Good afternoon, men. I'm Master Sergeant McDonald. I'm the first sergeant for the Recondo School, and I'll be taking you over to your barracks to get you settled."

"*You're* going to take us?" Brown's words dripped with respect for the NCO. None of the five replacements needed to be told that senior NCOs didn't waste their time with recruits, especially *senior* Green Berets.

"Yes. The other cadre are all busy, and our new class doesn't start until tomorrow, so, yes, I'll take you over and show you around . . . do you mind, Private Brown?" McDonald read the soldier's name tag on his fatigue jacket.

"No, sir! Lead the way!" Brown waited and then followed behind the NCO.

Woods noticed that everything was painted a dark green and was clean. The latrines were also painted, and cement sidewalks led to the different buildings. The structures were basically the same as the ones back in Saigon and the An Khe base area, but everything was extremely neat.

McDonald read the replacements' thoughts and answered the unasked question. "We live good in the base area, and we work *hard* in the field. That sort of sums up any Special Forces operation. We don't *practice* suffering." The master sergeant pointed to a cluster of buildings. "Those are yours. Your sleeping quarters are to the left . . . showers and latrine are in the center, and your classrooms are to the right. All training companies are separate from each other."

"Why do you do that, Sergeant?" Barnett asked, and Woods noticed that for the first time since he'd known him, Barnett's voice had a touch of respect in it.

The sergeant's answer was given in the tone of voice that one professional would use when he talked to another. There was none of the newbee bullshit or the you're-just-a-dumb-replacement tone to his voice. "We've found out that segregating our classes makes it easier on everybody." The sergeant stopped in front of the barracks he had pointed out to the group. "Find yourself a bunk and put your gear on it. Remember the number stenciled on the ammo box above the bed and fall back out here so we can go over to the supply room and issue you some bedding."

Woods followed the group into the building and found an empty bed next to Barnett. He dropped his duffel bag down on the bedsprings and turned to go back outside.

Barnett spoke to him over his right shoulder. "I'm going to like training here!"

"Yeah, this is the best place I've seen so far in Vietnam!" Woods held the screen door open for Barnett. The master sergeant had lit up a cigarette while he waited for the five men to fall out.

"How many soldiers are in each class, Sergeant?" Woods asked.

"Sixty. We start a new class every two weeks." McDonald took a long drag from his cigarette.

"Are *you* a Recondo, Sergeant?" Barnett looked the senior sergeant directly in the eyes.

McDonald read through Barnett instantly and took his time answering his question. "*All* of the cadre in the Recondo School are Recondo-trained: also Ranger, *three* Special Forces MOS's, *and* all of them have served at *least* one year in combat. That includes our supply sergeant and mess sergeant." McDonald took another long drag on his cigarette, and Woods could see the scar on McDonald's underarm, where his sleeve was rolled up, that went from the palm of his hand up to his elbow. "What's your name, soldier?" Barnett didn't have a name tag sewn on his jacket.

"Spencer Barnett, Sergeant."

"Well, *Spencer* Barnett, I think you'll find everyone in this school to your personal liking. We don't allow phonies to join us, our mission is too important."

Woods noticed that the master sergeant wasn't intimidated by Barnett's hostile glares.

"Have you *killed* anyone?" Barnett accented the word.

McDonald chuckled and then reached over and lightly placed his hand on Barnett's shoulder. "A boy from South Carolina is normally raised to be a bit more tactful with his elders."

"How did you know I'm from South Carolina?" Barnett was genuinely surprised.

"I'd say a bit northeast of Spartanburg. . . ."

"How in the hell did you know that!"

"I trained for most of one summer up near Hogback Mountain. Your accent gave you away." McDonald squeezed Barnett's shoulder and let him go. "Now let's go over and draw your basic issue for the school so you can relax and enjoy the rest of the afternoon."

Barnett followed the master sergeant like a puppy dog over to the supply room. Woods had to struggle in order to suppress a smile; he had never seen the hard-core Barnett so taken in by an NCO.

Woods put his books and other material he had been

issued in the ammo box attached to the wall above his bed. He sipped from the can of soda that he had bought at the NCO club. The club was open all day long for anybody to use. Woods was surprised that beer and hard liquor were sold during the day. He noticed when he had bought the soda that the NCOs who were in the club were mostly drinking beer and talking about their assignments at A-camps and projects along the Cambodian and Laotian borders. Woods looked over at Barnett's bunk and noticed that his clothes were folded up on his cot. A shower before supper sounded good, and Woods slipped out of his dirty fatigues and wrapped an olive-drab towel around his waist for the short walk over to the shower room.

A towel was hanging from one of the hooks. He could hear water running and stepped over to the open door to see if it was Barnett inside. The breath caught in Woods's throat. Barnett was standing to one side of the shower head, shampooing his hair with his eyes closed. David could see the round burn marks that started at each of Barnett's knees on the inside of his thighs and went up to his crotch. They were spaced about two inches apart. The scars were old ones and had turned white with age. Woods couldn't help but notice that Barnett wasn't circumcised, and one of the quarter-sized, circular white scars could be seen covering the top of his foreskin. Barnett opened his eyes just as Woods turned to leave.

"Hey! A shower's a good idea!" Woods tried acting like he hadn't seen anything. "Mind if I join you?"

"Sure . . . lots of room in here." Barnett turned his back on Woods. "These are *real* showers, with all of the water you want."

"Special Forces people know how to do things right." Woods stepped under a shower head and turned it on. He let the water hit his face and thought about what could have made those horrible scars on Barnett. When Woods stepped to the side of the shower to soap down, he saw that Barnett was gone.

When Woods had finished getting dressed, he walked alone over to the mess hall. There was a line. He could see Brown and Kirkpatrick in the line, and Masters about three men behind them, but Barnett wasn't there. Woods took his time eating the excellent casserole and went back up to see if he could have seconds; instead of the cook being pissed at him, Woods noticed that the man was pleased over the request for more. The second helping took longer to eat, and Woods thought about the shower incident. The scars were too uniform to have been an accident.

Barnett wasn't back at the barracks when Woods returned, and he started getting worried about him. Master Sergeant McDonald had told the group that there was going to be a movie set up behind the NCO club as soon as it got dark, and Woods decided on catching it before he went to bed, knowing that the next day a lot of hard training would begin.

Barnett sat in the corner of the NCO club sipping from a glass of straight bourbon. The corner was the darkest place that he could find. He was brooding. He had gone through basic training and AIT without having anyone see him in the showers. It had been very difficult, but he had done it. The doctor who had examined him at his induction physical had believed his story about a farm accident with a raking machine. The doctor was ready to believe anything. It was the long wait out in the sun that afternoon that had forced him to act so stupidly! When he saw the showers, he just couldn't wait until late at night when everyone else was asleep. He had weakened and tried showering in the daylight when, of all people, David Woods had walked in on him!

Woods went over to the dimly lit bar and ordered another

Shasta orange soda; he was beginning to think that he was addicted to the great-tasting drink. Barnett saw Woods first, drained his glass so he could leave, and then thought better of it. He was going to have to spend the next three weeks with Woods, and then maybe they would draw different assignments and he would be rid of him. He decided to gut it out.

"Mind if I join you?" Woods pointed to the chair across from Barnett.

Spencer shrugged his shoulders. "I was about ready to leave, anyway. Help yourself."

Woods took the seat and stretched out his legs sideways, away from the table. "I think that I should have gone into Special Forces."

Barnett didn't comment.

Woods continued talking. "They're probably the best soldiers we've got in Vietnam. Of course, I don't have enough rank. I think you have to be a buck sergeant."

"My stepfather did it," Spencer said, ignoring what Woods was saying and speaking in a low voice. "They're burns from his cigar. When I was a little shit, I wet the bed. He thought that if he burned me down there, I would stop wetting the bed."

Woods acted like he hadn't heard a word and talked right through the confession. "Do you think if I made buck sergeant, they'd let me join Special Forces?" Woods stood up. "What are you drinking . . . bourbon?"

Spencer nodded.

David went back to the bar and ordered three double bourbons and poured all of the drinks into one glass before returning to the table where Barnett sat alone.

"I don't know what went wrong in my life. I'm middle-class, smart . . . well a little *smart*." Woods dropped back down in his chair. "But look at you . . . a dumbass Southerner and you end up a slightly better soldier than I am. I mean, *five* points higher on the rifle range makes you an *expert*!"

Barnett smiled.

"Mind if I join you guys?"

Woods turned in his seat and saw Master Sergeant McDonald standing there. "Sure, Sergeant!"

McDonald took an empty chair and sat down. He didn't mince his words. "You seem to be drinking a lot, Barnett. Tomorrow's going to be a *long* day."

Barnett pushed the full glass of bourbon away from him. "I've already decided to change what I'm drinking... Shasta *orange* sounds good!"

Woods smiled.

For the rest of the night, the conversation around the table was Recondo tactics. McDonald enjoyed talking to the pair of young soldiers as much as they enjoyed listening to the veterans. Periodically throughout the evening, other sergeants who were cadre at the school, and some NCOs who were just visiting from the A-camps, would join them and talk for a while about the war and the different tactics they had used to get out of trouble, or new techniques the North Vietnamese were using in the jungles. Woods and Barnett were learning more about the war just listening at the table than they would have by serving six months in the field with a line unit.

Woods waited until there was a break in the conversation and they were alone with McDonald before he asked a question that had been bothering him all day. "Sergeant McDonald, why are the NCOs allowed to come in here during the day and drink?"

McDonald smiled. "None of the men you see in here during the day are working; in fact, most of them are from the A-camps along the borders and from the Greek Projects. The camps send back a couple of their men every so often for a few days off, and they visit here and at the main Nha Trang clubs. If you noticed, a lot of information is passed between SF units over a table in the bar, and no one gets drunk."

Woods nodded his head in agreement; he hadn't seen anyone drunk in the club.

"Well, it's going to be a long day tomorrow, and I need some sleep." McDonald got up to leave the table.

"Thanks." Barnett smiled.

"For what?" The master sergeant frowned.

"For talking to us." Barnett blushed. He was a little embarrassed.

McDonald shook his head from side to side. "That's my *job*. And it doesn't end at five o'clock."

The bright perimeter lights threw off enough light to see by on the sidewalks. McDonald decided on checking the training company barracks one last time before turning in himself. He entered through the back doors and walked down the aisle. Most of the men were already sleeping; the luxury of hot showers and soft cots were too good to miss. He saw Barnett and Woods slip in the front door and nodded to them. He waited until he was outside before shaking his head in total wonder; who would be dumb enough to send five raw replacements directly to a Recondo School? The message that the school had received earlier in the day that five new arrivals in-country would be assigned to the school from the 1st Cavalry Division was given to him by the school commandant, and he was ordered to personally insure that they were taken care of during the whole three weeks. McDonald was a professional soldier and was going to give it his very best shot. He lit up a cigarette and stood next to the barracks and smoked it while he thought. If the other three were as sharp as Barnett and Woods were, then his job would be easy. He shook his head again. Barnett couldn't be much over seventeen years old.

McDonald grumbled under his breath. "This fucking war!" He didn't mind serving; that was his job, but sending kids over was almost criminal.

The latrine lights were burning, and McDonald stopped under the glow from one of them and looked at his watch; it was a little after ten. He opened the door and went over to the nearest booth. The door was still a little sticky from the fresh coat of light green paint. The whole latrine smelled of paint thinner. He latched the door and took a seat on the commode. A message had been written in bold letters on the door at eye level: I KILL HONKIES!

McDonald knew that a detail had just finished painting the latrine that afternoon. The person who wrote the message had to be one of the men assigned to the new company, and all of them had just arrived the day before and during that afternoon. He left the latrine and walked over to the supply room. A table of NCOs were playing poker in the back room with the supply sergeant. McDonald waved but didn't join them. He went over to the small card file in which the troops had recorded their bedding issue and removed all of the new three-by-five cards where each man had printed out what he had drawn from the supply room. McDonald returned to the booth in the latrine and matched each bedding card against the message on the door. He eliminated all but two of the cards. One was a perfect match, and another a very close one.

The new trainees were woken up an hour before daylight and given time to shower and eat breakfast before the first formation. Master Sergeant McDonald was waiting for the men to fall out. He was getting more angry with each passing hour as he thought about the message on the latrine door. He was hoping that it was just a joke or some scare tactic of some weird sort. The bedding cards didn't reflect races, so he had to wait and see who the soldiers were during the formation.

Barnett saw McDonald standing near the barracks and waved a friendly greeting to the senior sergeant, who responded with a smile and a curt nod of his head. The men were falling out of the barracks wearing the normal-issue jungle tiger-striped fatigues the Special Forces men wore in the field, with matching hats in the same black, green, gray, and white pattern. There were no name tags or markings of any kind on the jackets. The whole idea was to have the men think like a new team, rather than have them identify with their units and form small cliques.

McDonald waited until all of the men were standing in ranks before he approached the duty NCO and handed him a note with the two names on it. He whispered to the sergeant that he wanted both of the men to report to his office immediately and left the formation.

The duty sergeant looked at the note and called out the two names. "*Fillmore! James!* Report to the orderly room and Master Sergeant McDonald!"

The two men fell out of the formation and walked the short distance to the orderly room for the Recondo School. McDonald watched through his screened window. One of the men was black and the other was white.

"Fillmore?"

"Yes, Sergeant!"

"Come in here." McDonald held his door open and beckoned for the young soldier to enter.

Fillmore took a seat and twisted his head around so that he could see the senior NCO. "Is something wrong, Sergeant?"

"Nothing serious. I just want to ask you a couple of questions." McDonald stared directly into the young soldier's eyes. "Where are you from back in the States?"

"Mississippi, Sergeant."

"Billy-Bob? Is that what you go by?"

"Yes, Sergeant . . . all my life."

"Do you hate blacks, Billy-Bob?" McDonald kept watching the soldier for a reaction. The young man blinked and pouted his lips slightly before answering the senior NCO.

"Not 'specially. Do you have someone in particular I should hate?"

"No . . . just in general."

"I might be from Mississippi, but that don't mean I have-ta hate anybody in *general*."

McDonald noticed a gold Christian cross hanging around the soldier's neck. "You a Baptist?"

Fillmore frowned over the question. "Pentecostal."

"You can return back to your class." McDonald lit up a cigarette. "They should still be in formation. Send in James."

The door opened, and Specialist Fourth Class Mohammed James stepped into the sergeant's office. He was wearing a knit black, red, and green skullcap on his head.

"Take a seat, Specialist." McDonald pointed at the chair. James hesitated just long enough to let the sergeant know that he sat down 'when *he* wanted to and not when told. "Been in Vietnam long?"

James glared at the sergeant before answering. "Fifteen months!"

"Second tour or a six-month extension?"

"Second tour!"

"Did you go home on leave?"

"Yeah!"

"Where's home?"

James licked his upper lip and didn't answer.

"I've got a problem, Specialist James." McDonald made his fingers into a tent on the desk in front of him and pressed his left upper arm against the cool steel of the pistol he carried in a shoulder holster under his loose-fitting fatigue jacket. "It seems that someone wrote a message on one of our latrine doors that I don't particularly like." McDonald could see James's eyes hood and a slight tightening of the muscles in his jaws. The senior sergeant had been a part of too many interrogations of enemy prisoners not to have noticed the tension in the black soldier sitting across from him. "Do you know anything about it?"

There was a very long pause before James looked at McDonald. A glare of pure hate was released before the words. "Naw . . . I don't know shit!"

McDonald smiled and leaned forward in his chair. "Do *you* kill honkies?"

James raised his eyebrows and smiled before he sneered at the sergeant. "I'm here to learn Recondo techniques. You teach and I learn. . . ."

"It says here that you're assigned to the 3rd Brigade of the 1st Cavalry Division. You with the Recon Company?"

"Not yet!" James stood up. "But I plan to be!"

"Go on back to your class." McDonald looked James directly in the eyes. "Don't plan on killing any honkies in my school . . . *friend*!"

James paused in the doorway and looked back over his shoulder. "Don't call me *friend*, Sergeant."

McDonald watched the door close. He wondered if James was just playing a game, but he didn't plan on taking any chances. He remembered hearing rumors that a group of Black Panthers were killing white soldiers during firefights in the 4th Division, but they were just rumors.

The first two weeks of Recondo School passed by very quickly for Barnett and Woods. It was obvious that the two of them were competing for the honor graduate position in the class, along with Mohammed James. The last week would be a seven-day patrol in the jungles surrounding Nha

Trang where they would put to the test all of the techniques they had learned in the classroom.

Barnett lay on his cot with his fingers laced behind his head. "Do you think we'll run into any Vietcong on patrol?"

"Who knows! This *is* Vietnam." Woods adjusted the straps on his pack and lifted it off his bed. He shook the bundle to see if there were any rattles coming from the pack. "The last class got three kills up on the mountains south of here."

"The instructor said that we're going to be inserted by helicopter about eight miles from here. There's a bridge and a large rice field north of it." Barnett rolled over on his side.

"We might run into some VC . . . if they're harvesting the fields at night." Woods felt a lump in his stomach.

"What instructor do you think we'll get?" Barnett was hoping for a good one.

"We should know in a few hours. The teams will be posted on the bulletin board." Woods checked his ammo pouches and adjusted the straps. He wanted everything to be perfect. Barnett was nine points ahead of him for honor graduate, and James was three points ahead. He couldn't afford any gigs on his gear for the patrol.

"If we capture a prisoner, we get a seven-day R and R to Australia and five hundred dollars to spend!" Barnett sat up on his cot.

"Don't hold your breath, partner!" Woods laughed.

"Do you think they'll put us on patrol together?"

"I don't know about you, but I hope *not*. I want some good men around me!"

"You fucking bastard!" Barnett dove at Woods and caught him around the waist. "I'm going to kick your ass!"

Woods was laughing too hard to fight back. "Get off me! Save your energy for the VC!"

Barnett pretended he was cutting Woods's throat with his finger and made a slicing sound.

"You white boys fuck around a lot. . . ." James passed by their bunks.

Barnett glared at the black.

"You seem to have an attitude problem, white boy." James stopped and looked down at Barnett, who was still on top of Woods. "Don't you like black people?"

Woods squeezed Barnett's wrist. "Not here, Spencer. They'll throw you out of this school."

"Don't fuck with black folk over here, Southern boy, 'cause we's gots *guns* and we ain't afraid to use them!"

James looked up and saw McDonald standing in the doorway watching him. He smiled at the senior sergeant and walked back to his bunk at the end of the barracks. McDonald stood watching for a couple of seconds and then left the building without speaking to anyone.

The clerk from the orderly room pushed the thumbtacks into each corner of the roster that listed each of the patrols for the week-long exercise. He hadn't finished the last thumbtack before there were trainees looking over his shoulder.

Woods saw the cluster of troops around the bulletin board and shook Barnett awake by grabbing his boot. "The roster's posted."

Barnett wiggled in between a couple of trainees and looked down the list. He saw his name surrounded by four others.

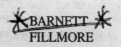

BARNETT
FILLMORE

JAMES
WOODS
TAYLOR
Team Leader: MSG McDONALD

"Holy fuck! McDonald's our Recon Team Leader!" Barnett scurried back out of the pack to where Woods waited for him.

"McDonald?" David was surprised. "He never goes out anymore. I asked earlier if we could be assigned to him, and the instructor told us that he had been shot up really bad when he was assigned to CCN and he didn't go out in the field anymore."

"His name's on the roster!" Barnett was happy. He had really grown to like McDonald over the past two weeks.

"I don't know about you, but I'm going back to check my gear again." Woods knew that the senior sergeant would be extra hard on him and Barnett because it had become common knowledge that the NCO liked them.

Woods lay awake on his bunk. He hadn't even gotten undressed. The bright moonlight filtered in through the screened window, along with a soft breeze coming off the South China Sea. The heavy plywood shutter shook a little and rattled the steel hook that normally locked it in place against the side of the building. They would be leaving in the morning on their first combat patrol. He wasn't scared, just nervous a little over facing the unknown. The war would start for him in the morning. Master Sergeant McDonald had checked all of their gear right after supper and assigned Barnett and Fillmore to the M-60 light machine gun. He had been given one of the new CAR-15s to carry during the recon mission and was happy with the selection. All of them had test-fired over fifty different weapons during their training, and he liked the CAR-15 the best. McDonald had personally insured that he and Barnett knew how to operate all of the North Vietnamese small arms, including the Russian pistols. The sergeant had reinforced in him that he would never be without a weapon or out of ammo if he knew how to operate the enemy's weapons. It made good sense.

Woods smelled smoke, turned his head, and saw the red tip of a cigarette burning at the far end of the hootch. James was awake also. Woods wondered what made him tick. It was obvious that James hated whites as much as Barnett hated blacks. That thought made him nervous, knowing that both of them would be on the same recon mission. The only good thing about it was that McDonald would be there.

Woods didn't know when he finally fell asleep. The hootch door opening woke him up. Two of the sergeants from the Recondo School walked down the aisle waking the trainees up by gently tapping the frames of their bunks; no one was sleeping heavily. The latrine was quiet as the men put their camouflage paint on their faces. Barnett used a tiger-stripe design and drew a set of black fangs at the corners of his mouth that reached down to the bottom of his chin. Woods smiled when Barnett looked at him and shook his head.

The sun was bright when they lined up next to the helipad for their final inspection by their recon leaders. McDonald took his time checking each one of his men. He gave Barnett five demerits for his camouflage makeup but grinned, anyway. There was a long pause when McDonald reached James, and the two of them stared at each other before the sergeant checked the soldier's gear. Woods sensed that there was something going on between the two of them, but he couldn't quite put his finger on it.

McDonald finished his inspection and lit up a cigarette. It would be the last one he would smoke for seven days. "Relax . . . we've got a couple of minutes before the choppers fire up. Remember, no talking once we insert, and whispering *only* in emergencies! I want a good deployment!" McDonald sat down on the warm PSP and leaned his back against his pack. He watched James.

Woods sat in the open door of the UH-1D Iroquois and looked down at the river they were flying over. Fishing boats and barges loaded with sacks of rice moved slowly toward the large city of Nha Trang at the mouth of the river. Master Sergeant McDonald had told them that the flight time from the Recondo School helipad to the field site would be only a few minutes. Woods felt the muscles around his rectum tighten, and a sour taste filled his mouth. He knew he was scared. Woods looked over at the other men riding in the helicopter with him. James sat with his back to him and he couldn't see his face, but Woods could see James's hand, and he was flicking the safety switch on and off on his M16. Fillmore carried extra ammo for the M-60 he was teamed with and an M-79 grenade launcher. He kept changing the round in the launcher from HE, high explosive, to a new flechette round that contained over fifty small darts about the size of a tenpenny nail with fins. McDonald had brought a case of the experimental rounds with him when he had left Command and Control North. The senior sergeant sat calmly, leaning out of the aircraft looking for their landing zone. Barnett glanced over at Woods and smiled. He had been waiting a long time for the opportunity to fight and was probably the only one on the Huey who was hoping the enemy would be waiting for them when they landed. The odds were against Barnett's wish. The Recondo School had selected the training reconnaissance patrols very carefully, so that there would be no major action. The area that they were going to patrol was a major rice-producing valley that fed the majority of the population around Nha Trang. A very well-trained Vietnamese Civilian Force and a battalion of South Vietnamese regulars patrolled the valley and the low-lying hills. The recon training team was being inserted just to the north of the valley, well within range of supporting fires from the friendly ARVN artillery units.

The helicopter touched down lightly on the blown-down elephant grass. Woods slipped out of the chopper and found out that he sank another three feet in the tall grass before his feet touched solid ground. He ran away from the chopper and dropped down to one knee with his CAR-15 pointed toward a thick line of trees twenty meters away.

The Huey backed away from the hillside and left. It became quiet . . . totally quiet . . . so quiet that Woods could *hear* the fear hiding in his stomach. He looked around for McDonald and saw him waving for the team to assemble. The movement when Woods ran to join up with the team felt good; it forced the fear to hide again. McDonald tapped each of the men on their shoulders and pointed to where he wanted them to go. He tapped Fillmore twice, which signaled that he would be the point man, followed by Barnett with the machine gun. McDonald nodded, and Fillmore moved out to the thick line of trees.

Woods was the rear guard and turned constantly in a half-circle to insure that the recon patrol wasn't ambushed from behind. He was just inside of the trees and felt a little more secure when the M-60 machine gun opened fire. David felt the crotch of his pants get warm from the urine. He had been caught off-guard, even though he was extremely alert. The sound of the automatic weapon had startled him.

McDonald had been caught off-guard also, but his reaction was different; he rushed past James and Taylor to reach the point man and Barnett. The machine gun broke the silence again with four series of six- to eight-round bursts, just like the book said to fire the light machine gun. McDonald noticed that Barnett was moving away from them each time the gun sounded. He felt fear and hoped that Barnett and Fillmore hadn't stumbled on a friendly local-forces patrol and mistaken them for Vietcong. Suddenly McDonald broke through the underbrush onto a hidden trail. The canopy formed by the trees had completely closed over the three-foot-wide path. Five North Vietnamese soldiers lay evenly spaced on the red-earth path. McDonald could see the sandaled feet of another NVA sticking out from the edge of the jungle. Fillmore was in the prone position just past the last dead NVA, his M-79 pointed down the trail.

McDonald dropped down by his side. He could see that the young soldier was almost in shock. He touched Fillmore's shoulder and spoke softly. "Where's Barnett?"

"Oh, shit, Sarge!" The relief was clearly evident in the young soldier's voice. "He's chasing a couple of NVA down the trail!"

"Chasing them?" McDonald was astonished.

"Yeah!"

The sound of an M16 barking to their rear brought McDonald and Fillmore around. The M-60 answered down the trail. Woods broke through the brush, followed seconds later by James. McDonald waved them into a defensive position and used his radio to call back to the base area for a reaction force. The Recondo School had made arrangements with the Special Forces headquarters in Nha Trang to have one of their Nung Mobile Strike Force Companies on strip alert when the Recondo School had trainees in the field. The Mobile Strike Force Company had never been used since the school had been established, until now. Six North Vietnamese in an area where they had never been sighted before was enough reason to activate the force as far as McDonald was concerned.

"Where's Taylor?" McDonald leaned over James but kept his eyes scanning the trail and the jungle.

"Still in the jungle. We saw a couple VC." James's voice was slightly muffled as he spoke, looking down.

Barnett appeared on the trail. Fillmore nearly shot him with a flechette round from the M-79. He had been so scared during the short encounter that he had forgotten to fire even one round. Less than five minutes had passed from the touchdown of the chopper to Barnett's reappearance.

McDonald waved for Barnett to join him. "What happened?"

Barnett dropped down next to the senior sergeant with his back facing in the opposite direction. "When we broke out on this trail, they were just turning around that bend"—Barnett pointed—"with their backs to us."

McDonald heard the sound of the helicopters just as a voice came over his radio asking for landing instructions. He nodded at Barnett and waved for the team to secure the area. He took Woods with him and went back the short distance to the landing zone and directed in the Mobile Strike Force's first platoon. The American sergeant who led the force took over the task of securing the area, and McDonald joined his recon team. Within an hour the rest of the Nung Mobile Strike Force had landed and formed a defensive circle around the area.

Taylor was still missing, and McDonald was worried that the man might have gotten separated from the patrol during the brief firefight. A Nung patrol returned carrying three NVA bodies. Barnett hadn't missed. The total kill was nine North Vietnamese regulars, and all of them were confirmed kills for one man: Barnett.

The American sergeant who led the Nung Company

dropped down next to McDonald. He wore a grim expression on his face. "We found your man. He's dead."

McDonald flexed his jaw. He was angry. He did not take losing his men lightly, and losing a trainee was even worse. McDonald turned his head and saw James staring at him. The look in the man's eyes gave him away. "I want to see the body."

"We've got him wrapped in a poncho on the LZ." The junior sergeant looked at McDonald as if he had gone off his rocker.

"Don't ship him out until I get there; first I want to check out these NVA for documents." McDonald beckoned Barnett and Woods over to him. "Search them thoroughly. Unbutton their shirts and pants and check for items taped to their skin. . . ." He saw the pistol belt and the red collar tabs and knew that the second NVA was an officer. McDonald went over to the body and personally searched it. The man was carrying a full leather pouch over his shoulder. McDonald lifted him up and removed the document carrier, placing it on the trail while he continued searching the body for anything that could be useful to the intelligence people. He removed the soldier's collar tabs, pistol belt, and wallet. McDonald made notes in his green, Army-issue notepad on the condition of the uniforms and even recorded small comments about the cleanliness of the bodies and uniforms, the condition of the NVA equipment, the physical condition of the soldiers before they died, and anything else that he thought the intelligence community could use.

Woods had joined McDonald just as the sergeant opened the fat leather pouch the NVA officer had been wearing over his shoulder.

"Holy shit!" Woods whispered the words between his clenched teeth.

Master Sergeant McDonald reached in and pulled out

one of the bundles of American hundred-dollar bills. "Now you know where all of this *green* money is going when you think you're getting over by trading a hundred dollars green for three hundred dollars of MPC. . . ."

"I wouldn't do that, Sergeant!" Woods was serious, he wouldn't, but McDonald knew a lot of his contemporaries who did exchange green dollars for MPC downtown for a profit.

"Barnett caught a courier detail taking money back up north. Looks like a couple hundred thousand dollars are in this pouch. No wonder they tried running rather than fighting." McDonald looked down the trail where Barnett lay resting. The young soldier smiled when his favorite sergeant looked at him. "They were finance people, not infantry."

"Are these guys NVA . . . *regulars*?" Woods stared at the dead officer.

"Yes."

James joined the sergeant and Woods. He had been watching, and when he saw the sergeant reach in the leather pouch and remove a bundle of American money, he became very interested. "You know, Sergeant, we could split that loot up between us and nobody would know the difference. . . ."

McDonald glared at James before he spoke. "*I* would." He shoved the money back in the pouch. "Our intelligence people can draw a lot of information from these bills and their serial numbers. Maybe we can catch the bastards who are supporting the North Vietnamese war effort!"

"What do you mean by that shit, Sergeant?" James's voice mocked the senior NCO.

"What I mean *is*, when a GI sells his green dollars to what he thinks is a whore, he's supplying the North Vietnamese with much-needed international currency that they use to buy weapons from China and Russia. Their money

ain't worth shit! They need American dollars or gold."
McDonald sealed the pouch and slipped it over his
shoulder. "Let's go back to the LZ."

"Are we leaving, Sergeant?" Barnett joined them.

"Yes."

"I thought this was a seven-day patrol!" Barnett was
pissed.

McDonald stopped walking and turned around to look at
the seventeen-year-old. "You fucking amaze me!"

Barnett beamed with pride. He took the remark as a
compliment, along with the first time he had heard the
master sergeant curse.

The helicopter ride back to the Recondo School was almost cheerful. Woods sat in the open door and enjoyed
watching the people below him and waved back at the kids
who waved up to the chopper from the backs of their water
buffalo.

The school commandant and five officers from the Special Forces headquarters were waiting for them when they
arrived. The recon team was escorted into a special de-
briefing room where the contents of the leather pouch were
emptied out on a table and counted. There were two
hundred and fourteen thousand dollars wrapped neatly in
ten-thousand-dollar bundles. A few twenty-dollar and ten-
dollar bills were in the bundle, but the vast majority of the
bills were new, American one-hundred-dollar notes. The
best discovery of all was a small package of receipts from
the people who had collected the money and exchanged it
for the NVA. One of the receipts was from a large bank in
Nha Trang that was obviously a front for the North Vietnamese. The receipt had been made out to the president of
the bank. The intelligence team was having a field day
with the contents of the pouch; it was also obvious that the
NVA major who had been killed had made the collection

trip so often that he had become careless, both with the material he carried and with his life.

Master Sergeant McDonald released the team and left in his jeep. He didn't tell anyone where he was going. The drive to the military mortuary at Nha Trang airfield was only a few minutes away. He had to know something, and he couldn't wait until the next day to find out.

Private Billy-Bob Fillmore was singing a popular Christian ballad in the showers when Woods entered the steamy building. Three piles of clothes were stacked on the benches outside the shower room. Woods placed his towel near the doors and sat down to remove his boots and socks. He entered the shower carrying a bar of soap and wearing the shirt and pants of his camouflaged tiger suit.

Barnett looked over at his friend and smiled. He couldn't care less now who saw the cigar scars. "Do you know how to shut this guy up?" He nodded at Fillmore.

Woods stood under a shower head and soaped down his uniform. "Sounds pretty good to me!" The comment encouraged the Bible Belt Pentecostal to sing louder.

James glared over at the three white soldiers, especially the one singing Christian songs in the shower. His entry stopped Fillmore from singing, and the tenor left the shower room.

"Hey, Woods! Did you fucking piss your pants out there today?" James's eyes matched his mocking voice.

Woods didn't hesitate in his answer. "Sure did! It scared the shit out of me!"

James did not expect Woods's answer; he thought Woods would deny it.

"Hey, James!" Barnett yelled loud enough to be heard outside of the shower room. "You sure have a small dick for a nigger!"

The big black soldier glared at Barnett and took an aggressive step toward him before he stopped himself. "You're walking *dead* meat, honkie . . . dead meat!"

Barnett tapped Woods on his shoulder and left the showers. Woods rinsed off his uniform and then took it off and twisted the water out of it before joining Fillmore and Barnett in the drying room.

"He's trouble." Woods nodded his head. "That guy *hates* whites more than you do blacks, Barnett . . . both of you had better back off!"

"No one pimps my friends!" Barnett's words were spoken from between clenched teeth.

"I can handle myself. It was true!" Woods shrugged his shoulders. "I pissed my pants."

"Let's get some food!" Fillmore ended the conversation by starting to sing another Christian hymn. He looked over at the shower-room doorway and sang louder.

"You know, you're not half bad." Barnett patted Fillmore's shoulder, and the three of them left together for the mess hall. "Hey, Woods! Do you think Sergeant McDonald will let us go back out in the field tomorrow?"

Woods slapped Barnett on the back of his head. "You *are* fucking crazy!"

McDonald had returned from the military mortuary with the information he needed. He went over to the supply area and checked the weapons that had been taken off the NVA soldiers; none of them had been fired recently. He had enough information to go to the school commandant.

James left the shower room angry. He had fucked up and knew that he was in big trouble. No one had seen him shoot Taylor, but he had acted too early in the contact with the enemy. He blamed himself, but how was he to know that the NVA wouldn't fire back at the recon team, or that the rest of his team had been too taken by surprise to fire their weapons. When he had been in a line unit, it had been much easier. If one man opened fire, the whole platoon fired for at least a couple of minutes. It had been easier back then, but now he just had to be more careful.

McDonald stood outside of the commandant's door and took a deep breath; he didn't know how the lieutenant colonel was going to take what he had to say because even though the officer was a well-qualified member of the Special Forces, he was black.

The commandant listened quietly to what McDonald had to say. The only emotion he showed was a slight tapping of his finger against his lips when he heard something he particularly found offensive. He waited until McDonald had finished his briefing before commenting, "You have made some good observations, Sergeant, and I tend to agree with you. We have a *real* problem here!"

"Yes, sir."

"How we handle it is going to be difficult." The lieutenant colonel was worried. The topic was extremely explosive and could cause a great deal of harm to the American troops fighting in Vietnam. Black soldiers killing whites on the battlefield was a *very* heavy topic. "We must be sure . . . very sure."

"Sir, Taylor was killed by an M16 rifle. None of the NVA carried captured American weapons. Only one man on my team fired his weapon, and that was an M-60. James was alone with Taylor when it happened and said two NVA carrying M16s ran back through the jungle. I personally checked the area and found only four empty rounds, and they were very near to the spot James had been at. Sir, that's a lot of circumstantial evidence!" McDonald shifted in his seat. "And when you add in the message on the latrine door. . ."

"I know, I know..." The lieutenant colonel stood up and walked over to his screened window. "Just trust me, McDonald, I have to be very sure! I hope you understand how much this bothers me! I've busted my ass to make lieutenant colonel, and to be honest with you, I want to wear stars someday. I...I...Christ! How in the hell can he do it!" The officer was in a rage. "Kill his fellow Americans!"

"I understand, sir."

"Prepare a message for the 3rd Brigade Commander over at the 1st Cavalry Division. Detail what we know and I'll have it sent to him, for his eyes only." The commandant tapped his lip with his right index finger. "He graduates from here shortly. We won't have time to do much, and I don't want to act so fast that he gets away. If he is killing his fellow soldiers, I want his ass to hang!"

"Yes, sir, I'll have it ready in the morning."

"Oh, McDonald..."

"Yes, sir?"

"Private Barnett is going to receive an impact award tomorrow from the 5th group commander...right after breakfast."

"Excellent, sir...excellent." McDonald left the headquarters building and walked slowly over to the NCO club in the dark. He needed a stiff drink.

James stood in the shadows and watched the sergeant leave the commandant's office. His eyes were narrowed into slits.

Barnett had no idea what was going on at the morning formation. All of them had been told that they would be shipping out early to their units. The 3rd Brigade was still in a big fight in the Ia Drang Valley and was begging for replacements.

"What do you think the 5th group commander wants

over here?" Barnett whispered to Woods as they waited for the colonel to come out of the commandant's office.

"Got me. Probably wants to say good-bye or good luck." Woods watched the screen door to the commandant's office.

"Here he comes," Fillmore said to the whole group.

The 5th group commander walked straight over to where the small group of trainees and instructors stood and stopped directly in front of McDonald. A captain followed the colonel, carrying a velvet pillow with a Silver Star Medal pinned in it.

"Private Spencer Barnett . . . fall out!"

Barnett was caught by surprise but obeyed. The colonel pinned the award on the young soldier's jacket and shook his hand. He stared at Barnett, then spoke. "How old are you?"

"Seventeen, sir!"

The gray-haired man nodded and turned to leave, followed by the school commandant. He murmured under his breath as he got into his jeep. "Babies! They're shipping us fucking babies to fight this war!"

The commandant saluted and quietly agreed with the colonel.

The Recondo School graduates who were leaving early for their units had already packed and had their gear lined up outside of their hootches for pickup. Woods saw McDonald walking across the open parade grounds toward them. Barnett scooted up against the building and looked down between his knees. He had hoped on missing having to say good-bye to the sergeant.

"What's he carrying?" Woods squinted to see better but could only make out two silver-and-brown packages, one under each of his arms.

"You got me." Barnett's voice gave away his feelings. "I wish he hadn't come."

"Hey! He *likes* you!"

"I know. That's why I wish . . ." Barnett didn't finish his sentence before McDonald saw them and walked over.

"You're hard to find!" McDonald grinned.

"Hi, Sergeant. We're getting ready to leave for Qui Nhon." Woods did the talking while Barnett continued looking down at his boots.

"Well, I brought you two something . . . special." He handed each one of them a canvas holster and a Browning 9-mm pistol.

"Holy shit!" Woods was surprised.

"They have fourteen-round magazines."

Barnett took the offered pistol but kept his eyes from meeting McDonald's. He knew that if he looked directly at the sergeant, he would start crying like a baby.

"There's more." He handed each of them one of the airtight brown packages and waited for them to tear them open. "Well, go ahead and open them! Now, these are *hard* to come by, but I couldn't let my two favorite Recondo students leave here without the proper equipment."

Barnett started opening his package, but he could feel the weapon inside and started blinking back the tears before it was open.

"Oh, *man*! A CAR-15!" Woods spoke loud enough for both of them. "Sarge, where did you get these?"

"That's my secret. There are only a very few of them in Vietnam right now . . . here." He handed them a folded piece of paper. "Just in case someone wants to take them away from you."

Woods opened the paper and saw that it was a weapons-issue slip from the Recondo School for a permanent loan.

"Well . . . I've got to get back to work." McDonald

turned to leave what was becoming an awkward situation. "New group of trainees coming in. . . ."

"Sarge?" Barnett's voice was choked with emotion.

"Yeah?" McDonald stopped.

Barnett hugged him. "Thanks."

"Shit! Stop that!" McDonald chuckled and grabbed Barnett's arms. He only hugged harder. "I'm going to lose my reputation as a hard ass!"

Woods stood there crying along with Barnett. He didn't give a fuck who saw him.

The sound of a truck's engine broke Barnett's hold on the sergeant's neck. Woods picked up his gear. Barnett wiped his eyes with his sleeve and went over to his pack and shoved the pistol inside. McDonald watched the men load up on the truck. He waited until the vehicle was pulling away from the building before he used his hand to wipe away the film covering his eyes.

Woods sat at the back of the truck with the new CAR-15 lying across his lap. Barnett tried smiling.

"Don't get yourself killed . . . hear?" McDonald grinned and watched the truck pull away for the helipad.

T H R E E

The Ia Drang Valley

The dust seemed to be waiting for any opportunity to jump up from the ground and seek refuge in a human throat or nostril. A man walking between the bunkers would cause a small cloud of the fine, red dust to roll along the ground, but the worst clouds were created by the helicopters that were constantly landing and taking off. An Khe was the base camp for the 1st Cavalry Division Airmobile, and the word *airmobile* meant hundreds of helicopters.

Lieutenant Reed sat outside of his hootch trying to clean his M16. He had the weapon disassembled on his poncho, but every time he had wiped it clean, a coating of the red dust covered the parts. It was useless trying to oil the working parts of the rifle. Reed sighed and waited for the dust to settle, and then he quickly brushed the parts off and reassembled the weapon before another helicopter landed. He wrapped the M16 up in his poncho and took it back into his hootch. He hated the dust more than the monsoon mud.

"That's almost a lost cause, Lieutenant."

Reed looked over and saw his platoon sergeant entering the hootch. "I know, but I try." Reed sat down on his folding cot. "Have the new replacements arrived yet, Sergeant Fitzpatrick?"

"They're due in this morning." The senior sergeant took a seat on the cot across from his lieutenant and reached into one of the side pockets of his jungle fatigues for his pouch and filled his pipe with the high-grade marijuana. He inhaled a couple of long tokes before offering the pipe to the lieutenant.

Reed looked out of the screened windows before taking the pipe. He didn't smoke that often and never smoked when he was in the field, but he wanted to let the men know that he was one of the guys. "I hope they fill up our teams. It's been quite a while since our platoon has been active in the field."

"They graduated three men from the Recondo School early, and we should be getting eight more after their field exercise is completed." Fitzpatrick took another long toke from his pipe. He was beginning to feel the effects of the drug. "Simpson's got his hands on some good stuff here." He handed the pipe back to the lieutenant.

"Yeah, but I've got to meet the replacements. . . ." Reed waved aside the offering.

Fitzpatrick leaned back on the cot and rested his head against the plywood wall. "I hear one of them earned a Silver Star when he was on his training patrol as an impact award, and the general is upgrading it to a Distinguished Service Cross."

"A DSC?" Reed didn't even try hiding the jealousy in his voice.

"He supposedly zapped nine NVA, and one of them was a major!" Fitzpatrick was impressed, and his voice showed it. "I could use him on my team."

"Arnason has first pick from the replacements." Reed

glanced over at his platoon sergeant, knowing that he was trying to pull a quick one over on him. "Let's keep it fair."

"Sure, Lieutenant, sure . . ." Fitzpatrick grinned. "I was just trying to form a good team, that's all." The last two words were slightly slurred. The sergeant was getting high.

Lieutenant Reed stood up and adjusted the tops of his jungle fatigues in his boots. "I've got to see the company commander about our mission in the Ia Drang." Reed looked over at his platoon sergeant with a flash of contempt in his eyes. He hated the sergeant's vices, and there were many of them, but the man was a superb soldier in the field. "Are you going to be here or at your hootch?"

Fitzpatrick stretched out on the empty cot. "I'll wait here for you, Lieutenant."

The Brigade Recon Company commander had his back to the bunker entrance when Reed entered the command post. A half dozen blue pins were stuck on the map, surrounded by twenty or thirty red pins. The captain was posting more sightings of enemy units on the map with the Brigade S-2 officer.

"Damn, sir! It looks like the whole Ia Drang Valley is full of NVA!" Reed joined the officers.

The captain spoke without looking at his lieutenant. "The 1st Brigade has taken a number of casualties. LZ X-Ray was almost overrun last night, but the cav troops held them off in hand-to-hand combat."

Reed felt the fear grip his stomach. It was times like this that he wished he would have stayed at Georgetown University and gotten his master's degree. He had enjoyed ROTC training and had even tolerated the harassment from the powerful antiwar movement on campus when he wore his cadet uniform; in fact, it was the harassment that had forced him to take airborne and reconnaissance training during the summers.

"If the 3rd Brigade is committed to the fight, your four

recon teams will be inserted south of the Ia Drang River to the rear of the Chu Pong Massif . . . here." The captain pointed to the large, flat plateau that straddled the South Vietnamese–Cambodian border. "They say there are two NVA regiments in the battle and that they're being resupplied from the Massif. The division commander wants to know for sure."

"Yes, sir." Reed swallowed. "I'm still short men."

"Not anymore." The captain nodded toward the company headquarters hootch. "You have three replacements waiting for you over in supply . . . they're drawing their equipment."

"Great, sir!" The words lacked enthusiasm.

Woods, James, and Barnett all sat on their packs in the supply tent. The structure was built out of two-by-fours and plywood with a GP large tent stretched over it to make it waterproof. Heat hung under the tent about head high. The strong odor of mothballs and preservatives identified the supply area, and the odor coming from the canvas tent almost drew the breath out of the new replacements' lungs. Barnett frowned ánd scooted over closer to the rolled-up, shady side of the structure.

Sergeant First Class Shaw sat behind the gray desk and read the weapons-issue slip from the Recondo School for the sixth time. He was pissed. Two of the new replacements carried experimental models of the M16 called CAR-15s. The weapon had the same firing mechanism as the M16, but the design changed in the telescoping stock and the round hand guards and shorter barrel. The flash suppressor was fatter and longer, also. What the CAR-15 looked like was a shorter, easier-to-handle M16. Shaw had heard that some of the new weapons were in-country, but only special units of the Special Forces were issued them for evaluation. How these two replacements had gotten hold of them was a mystery.

"Sorry, guys, this issue slip doesn't mean shit here in the Cav." Shaw waved the slip at Woods and Barnett. James smiled. "You're going to have to turn those weapons in and get issued regular M16s like everyone else!"

"But, Sarge, if we can't keep them, then we have to send them back to the Recondo School," Woods said, trying to reason with the sergeant.

"You do what in the fuck I tell you!" Shaw left his desk and came over to Woods, holding out his hand for the weapon. "Give it to me!"

"Bullshit!" The voice came from the entrance. Everyone in the tent turned to see who had spoken.

"You keep your fucking nose out of this, Arnason!" Shaw growled the words.

"Fuck you, Shaw!" Sergeant Arnason stepped all of the way into the supply tent. "You're not going to fuck those guys out of their weapons and then sell them to the highest bidder!"

"Are you calling me a fucking crook?" Shaw's face turned red.

"Yes."

"Get the fuck out of here!"

"When I get my men . . . and their equipment." Arnason rested his hand on the pistol he carried on his hip, which was in a leather NVA holster.

Shaw's eyes shifted from the CAR-15s to Arnason's hand. It wasn't worth getting in a fight over, especially with Arnason. He was fucking crazy. He would go to the captain and force the replacements to give up their CAR-15s through him. The worst that would happen was that the captain would want one of the new weapons, but he still would have one left to sell. He knew that he could get at least a thousand dollars, MPC, for it.

"I'll see you later, Arnason . . . with the captain!"

"Fine. Until then, asshole, issue these men their field gear." Arnason's voice remained even. He noticed that all three of the men wore Special Forces tiger suits and added, "They won't need jungle suits right now."

Arnason led the three replacements back to Lieutenant Reed's hootch and had them wait outside while he checked inside for the lieutenant. He found Fitzpatrick stoned on the bed.

"Fitz, I've got three of the replacements. Where do you want them to go?"

The platoon sergeant lifted his head from the cot and struggled to sit up. "Where . . . where are they?"

"Outside."

Fitzpatrick stumbled to the screened door and looked out. "Which one is the Silver Star winner?"

"You got me." Arnason took a step out of the door and called over to the waiting men, "Which one of you has a Silver Star?"

Barnett raised his hand.

"The blond-haired kid." Arnason was impressed.

"The lieutenant said you can have first choice."

"I'll take the kid."

Fitzpatrick looked out through the screen. The remaining two replacements sat looking out at the perimeter and couldn't see him looking at them. Slowly James turned and glared at the side of the hootch. Fitzpatrick smiled. "I'll take the black guy. He looks mean enough to kick a lot of ass."

"Fine. I'll take the other kid, and that will fill up my team." Arnason nodded and left the building.

Fitzpatrick relit his pipe and sat on the bed until the bowl was empty. He enjoyed staying stoned in the rear area and planned on getting drunk with his friend, the supply sergeant, as soon as it got dark.

Arnason stepped into the shade. "What's your name?"

"James."

"You're being assigned to Sergeant First Class Fitzpatrick's team. He's also the platoon sergeant, so don't give him any shit!" Arnason nodded with his head toward the hootch. "He's in there getting fucked up." He beckoned with his finger at Barnett and Woods. "You two come with me."

James entered the hootch, saw the sergeant leaning against the wall, and smiled. This was his kind of NCO. The sergeant held out the pipe for James to take after he drew in a lungful of the relaxing smoke.

James smiled and took the offered bowl.

Staff Sergeant Arnason led the way out to the perimeter. He stopped in the entrance of an eight-man fighting bunker and turned back to face the two new replacements. "This is going to be your home when you're in the base camp." Arnason entered the entrance through the zigzagged dirt and sandbag maze that protected the opening from direct fire and shrapnel.

Woods blinked his eyes in the soft light and waited while they adjusted. A soldier sat on one of the bunk beds that had been built into the wall.

"Sinclair, meet your new teammates, Woods and Barnett." Arnason nodded to the pair. "How about showing them around the area and getting them settled in? I've got to get briefed."

"No problem, Sergeant." Sinclair pointed at two empty bunks. "Take your pick."

Barnett dropped his pack on the nearest bunk and went over to the open firing slit and looked out over the field of fire the bunker commanded. "We're right on the perimeter."

"Yeah, they don't *waste* recon men!" Sinclair had the kind of voice that never offended anyone; if you didn't know him, you would think he was weak. "Actually, Sergeant Arnason is the only recon team leader who uses a fighting bunker for a rear-area hootch."

"Why?" Woods laid his CAR-15, wrapped in his poncho liner to keep the dust off it, on his pack.

"I'd better tell you now and save you a lot of grief. He doesn't believe in doing dope, getting drunk, or any of that kind of stuff. He's a real weird guy, but he's the best recon leader in the Cav! He's got us living out here to keep our *senses* sharp." Sinclair pointed to a vertical ladder that led to an opening in the roof. "Let's go up top, and I'll show you around the area from there."

Woods and Barnett followed Sinclair to the top of the twenty-by-fifteen-foot fighting bunker. Two plastic lawn chairs were placed near a stack of ammo boxes that were used for storage. Sinclair lifted the top of one of them and exposed a dozen M-26 hand grenades still in the cardboard packing tubes, and a dozen white phosphorus grenades.

Barnett took a seat on the three-foot-high wall that surrounded the top of the bunker. "Nice setup."

"It leaks a little during the monsoons, but it's drier than in the field." Sinclair pointed down the perimeter to another large fighting bunker. "We occupy every third bunker during the day with a topside guard. All of the fighting bunkers have to have at least one man in them at all times, and during the night four men at all times with two up top on guard."

"I noticed that only four bunks are occupied." David nodded back down the ladder.

"Arnason won't allow any of the rear-area people to live in our team bunker, except when we're in the field. Two of the company's rear-area clerks are detailed to help pull guard at night."

"This Arnason seems like a real weird character." Barnett tested the waters.

"Like I said before, he's the best recon leader in the Cav. He's a little weird, but when you think about it, he makes sense. Take, for example, his hang-up about air-conditioned buildings. He won't let any of us spend more than an hour in one of them, even back in Saigon or someplace like that."

"Why?" Woods frowned. "Is he crazy?"

"No, he thinks it screws you up, and when you're in the jungle, you won't be able to take the heat. That's why there's no smoking in this bunker . . . to keep your sense of smell sharp." Sinclair looked over at Woods out of the corner of his eye. "I hope, for your sake, you don't do dope."

"No need to worry about that shit!" Barnett's voice carried the message clearly to the recon man watching him. "I came here to kill gooks!"

Woods watched Sinclair for a reaction to the offensive term. He could see that the man was at least half Oriental.

"You'll have plenty of opportunity for that . . . maybe sooner than you've planned."

"How's that?"

"We're going to be deployed into the Ia Drang Valley very soon." Sinclair's voice lowered. "Now that we're full-strength, that might be *very* soon."

"Where's the Ia Drang?"

"It's a valley that borders Cambodia. The 1st Brigade's been fighting there for three weeks now and has taken a lot of casualties." Sinclair's eyes reflected his worry and concern. "It's the biggest battle of the war. They say the NVA have thrown three regiments into the fight and have already taken over a thousand KIA."

"What're our losses?" Woods asked.

"They say a couple hundred KIA and wounded, but it's more like three hundred KIA alone. That's why the 3rd

Brigade has been put on standby alert to relieve and reinforce them."

"What's with all of this *they*-say shit!" Barnett felt his stomach roll and covered the fear with his aggressive statement.

"*They* say because . . . I haven't been there . . . yet." Sinclair let the little blond-haired soldier know that he wasn't about to be intimidated.

"It looks like Sergeant Arnason is coming back." Woods pointed to the distant figure weaving his way between the wooden barracks.

"He's probably got news about our mission." Sinclair took a seat on the hot sandbags and reached down for a piece of cardboard to sit on. He watched quietly as the sergeant approached.

Arnason was inside of the bunker a good twenty minutes before he called the team in. A large map covered with a thin sheet of plastic had been tacked to the far wall. Large red and blue grease-pencil marks had been copied on the overlay, with a black square four kilometers on each side occupying the right edge of the battle area that had only red marks inside of it.

"That's our AO." Arnason tapped the black square on the map with his finger. "We're flying into Camp Holloway outside of Pleiku . . . tonight." He paused and looked over at Sinclair. "I'm going to have to depend on you a lot this time, Reggie."

"No sweat, Sergeant!" Sinclair flexed his jaw muscles.

"Two new men and a mission like this!" Arnason shook his head. He had tried talking the captain out of sending his team out so soon. He wanted to have time to take the new replacements out on a couple nighttime perimeter-shakedown missions first.

"We can carry our share, Sergeant!" Barnett's pride was hurt.

"Yeah!" Arnason said, then continued his briefing. "From Holloway we're going to be flown to a Special Forces A-camp on the border called Du-Co. It's a very hot camp . . . they've been under seige for over a hundred days so far, and from there we're going to walk in to our AO." Arnason's voice lowered when he spoke the last sentence.

"Walk in?" Sinclair shook his head. "Sarge! That's ten clicks before we even get to our AO!"

Arnason raised his eyebrows and lowered them. "Helicopters can't make it . . . they're getting shot down just flying into Du-Co."

"Damn!" Sinclair slapped a green metal ammo box.

"This is going to be a tough one . . . a tough one." Arnason sat down on a crate. "Listen up, we've got a lot to cover."

Barnett and Woods wore the same set of tiger fatigues they had arrived in on the insertion helicopter leaving from An Khe. The flight to Camp Holloway was at two thousand feet above small-arms range. The slick refueled at the large airfield and picked up a four-gunship escort out to Du-Co. They received ground fire three times during their low-level flight, with only a half dozen rounds hitting the Huey. The pilot touched down only for a couple of seconds inside of the A-camp and joined the circling gunships for the return flight back to Camp Holloway.

Arnason led his four-man recon team over to the side of a bunker where a Special Forces intelligence sergeant waited to escort them to the command bunker and a final briefing. Woods noticed the strained looks on all of the A-camp's occupants' faces. They had been under attack for a long time. A dozen mortar rounds impacted inside the camp's perimeter just as the recon team reached the underground bunker entrance. The NVA had been trying to hit the helicopters but had been too late in getting their firing data. A series of *plop-whooshes* of the SF mortars' returning fire followed the team down the steps.

"I don't know what side of the wire is safest!" the Green Beret NCO said, trying to make light of the mortar attack.

Arnason answered politely. "I prefer the jungle to this shit."

"I won't argue with that." The sergeant tapped the briefing board and went into the battle situation surrounding the two Special Forces A-camps that straddled the Ia Drang Valley. "We've been under siege for a couple of months now, and Plei Me, to the south, has been nearly overrun twice. There's been a change to your insertion orders. Instead of walking from here, you're going to be flown into LZ Mary. It's been opened up by the cav since yesterday evening. We think we can get you in there." The sergeant shook his head. "It's a *lot* better than trying to walk in from here." He looked at the faces of the three young recon men. None of them were older than nineteen, and the blond-haired kid looked like he was fifteen. The sergeant team leader was the only professional in the lot. He had tried talking the Cav intelligence people out of sending men on such a suicide mission. The Chu Pong Massif was the property of the North Vietnamese Army, and had been since the beginning of the battle.

"That solves part of my problem." Arnason saw the look in the Green Beret's eye. "When can we leave?"

"Now, if you like. There's a resupply chopper getting ready to go into LZ Mary, and we can add an extra Huey for your team."

"Let's do it." Arnason stuffed his map in the side pocket of his fatigues. He fought to keep a blank expression on his face, knowing that his men would sense any weakness in his leadership instantly. "Fall outside for a quick inspection." Arnason followed his men up the steps and quickly checked them out for any loose equipment that might rattle or make a noise of any kind. A lot of items were overlooked in a base camp. "Jump up and down."

Woods obeyed, followed by Barnett. Their gear was well taped and secured. Arnason was impressed.

The Green Beret intelligence sergeant came out of the bunker entrance carrying four thirty-round M16 magazines. He handed one to each of the recon men. "I hate parting with these—they're very hard to come by—but right now I think your team could use them more than I do. It's a *loan,* understand." The sergeant smiled. "I want them back someday, and don't worry about the load. I personally inspected each round."

"Thanks!" Barnett removed the twenty-round magazine from his CAR-15 and inserted the thirty-round one.

"A few extra rounds might make the difference, especially on a chance encounter..." The Green Beret felt a little bit better about letting the recon team go on their mission. He still wished that he could talk the cavalry intelligence people out of sending them.

"Yeah, this is great! Going from eighteen rounds to twenty-eight *will* make a difference!" Woods seated the new magazine in his CAR-15 and felt the weapon for balance. He never loaded his magazines to their full capacity, believing that if the spring was too compressed, it would jam rounds in the chamber.

"This is really kind of you." Arnason knew how rare the thirty-round magazines were, and the sacrifice the NCO was making for their sake.

"Like I said, they're on *loan*. I expect to have them back!" The sergeant waved as the recon team left to board the helicopter.

Landing Zone Mary was littered with stacks of mortar cardboard tubes and wooden cases. The four 81-mm mortars fired constantly out into the surrounding eight-foot-high elephant grass in support of the infantry companies that were fighting for their lives. The helicopter pilot's face was the last thing Woods remembered as the chopper pulled away, banked to the south, and burst into a ball of flames two hundred meters away from the base. Pieces of the chopper were scattered all over the ground. No one even attempted forming a rescue team, knowing that there were no survivors.

"The bastards just sit out there in the elephant grass and wait for the gunships to head on back ahead of the slicks, and then they zap one or two of them." The voice came from a very tired captain. "I've told them a thousand times to have their escort ships leave *last*!" The captain looked at the recon team wearing tiger fatigues. "You don't look like any Cav replacements to me."

"We're not, sir." Arnason identified himself as the team leader. "We're a recon team."

"A *recon* team?" The captain slapped his forehead with the palm of his hand. "And what in the fuck is a *recon* team doing here at LZ Mary!"

"We've been dropped off here so that we can walk into our AO, sir."

"And may I fucking ask where that AO is?" The captain's voice was filled with tired sarcasm. "We *know* where the enemy is, Sergeant." He swept his hand out to the west side of the camp and then turned and swept the other three directions. "Pick anywhere out there."

"I have a mission to recon the Chu Pong Massif."

"Do you fucking know what you're saying?" The captain was very angry. "The Chu Pong is where we think the NVA have their division headquarters. I'll say that again for any deaf ears . . . read my lips! Their *division* headquarters!" He pointed at Arnason. "You and your team will *not* be going out there, not just four of you!"

"Sir, I take my orders from my brigade commander."
Arnason spoke with respect, but he was firm.

"Your brigade commander hasn't been out here! If I send
you and your men out there, I'll be telling you to commit
suicide!" The captain pointed to a section of the LZ perimeter.
"Go over there and tell Lieutenant Hayes that you'll be
assigned to his perimeter until I can get you out of here!"

"Yes, sir." Arnason nodded for his team to join him. He
went over to the lieutenant and reported. They were given
two fighting holes that were empty. The lieutenant looked
relieved. He was short twelve men in his platoon and
hadn't received any of the promised replacements.

Woods and Sinclair were put in the same hole, and Arnason kept Barnett with him. He thought that it would be a
good time to learn something about his new man and Sinclair could break in Woods. Arnason and Woods dozed for
most of the afternoon and then relieved Sinclair and Barnett, so that they could get some rest between mortar and
rocket attacks from the NVA forces.

Three MEDEVAC choppers low-leveled into the LZ to
remove the company's wounded. Arnason was impressed
over the guts the chopper pilots showed coming in to the
base under heavy enemy fire.

Arnason saw the captain running toward his hole. He
stood up and waved the captain in. The hole was tight with
the three men packed in it, but to try talking outside of the
protection was inviting a sniper round.

"Bad news." The captain couldn't look Arnason directly
in the eyes. "I received a radio message. You're to exfil-
trate the LZ and recon your assigned area." The captain bit
his lip. "I tried . . . but division intelligence feels your mission is too important."

"No problem, Captain. I told you we were assigned a
hot mission."

"Well, I'll alert the perimeter guards so you won't get

shot by our own men. I'll also set it up so that you can sneak back in if things are too hot out there." The captain still couldn't look the sergeant in the eyes. "Set your radio on our freq, and two clicks on the handset will warn us that you're coming back in the same way you went out. Wait for three clicks before coming back through. Remember, we'll key the handset *three* times to let you know that it's all clear."

"Fine." Arnason was transforming into another human being. He was psyching himself up, and within a matter of minutes he would be a perfect killing machine.

Woods was terrified. He crawled slowly behind Arnason through the tall elephant grass. The team was close together in the thick undergrowth as they moved. Arnason took his time and stopped often to listen. Woods knew the rest of the team could hear his heart pounding; he could hear the drumbeats in his ears. Barnett followed him, and Sinclair brought up the rear. Woods was becoming more and more impressed with Sinclair; the man didn't say much, but he was always there.

Arnason stopped crawling and took three deep breaths of much needed air in order to calm down his nerves. He was scared. He knew that he would have to quickly gain control of his fear or the whole team would be in jeopardy. He smelled cigarette smoke and reached back and tapped Woods, who eased up next to him. Arnason pointed in the direction the faint odor came from and started crawling slightly away from it. He wanted to slip between the NVA positions that circled the landing zone and not make contact. The cigarette smoke was an excellent guide for Arnason. He guessed the location of the enemy position and crawled around it but still remained close enough so that he wouldn't run into a nearby fighting position. Once they had gone a good two hundred meters, Arnason stopped crawl-

ing and rested his team. They waited for an hour and then
moved to the southwest in a low crouch, carrying their
weapons at the ready. Woods felt a little better after they
started traveling on their feet. He could feel a slight burning sensation coming from his knees.

Daylight was a welcome friend even though the light
made it easier for them to be detected by the NVA. Arnason stopped his team when the sun was directly overhead
and signaled for them to form a defensive perimeter for a
long rest break. He had selected a thick stand of fifty-foot-
tall bamboo that would be unlikely for the NVA to bother
with when they could travel on the easier paths through the
high elephant grass. Arnason was amazed at how well the
NVA forces moved through the sparse cover. The whole
valley floor was a large bed of elephant grass six to eight
feet tall with trees scattered out over the valley floor as if a
giant had thrown a handful of seeds on the ground. Small
stands of bamboo grew near streams and wet spots in the
valley, but the preponderance of cover was the tall grasses.
Arnason had been worried all night long about a chance
encounter with a large snake. The terrain screamed of
cobra and python country. He had heard wild pigs all during the night rooting for food and knew that was also a sign
that tigers were around.

A small two-seater L-19 observation aircraft cruised directly over the recon team's position. The team could see
the white star painted on its sides and the large white letters
that spelled out ARMY. Woods thought that it took a lot of
guts for an observer to fly up there in the open. A stream of
green tracers, followed with the loud report of the heavy
machine gun, answered Woods's thought. The team instinctively ducked. The heavy weapon was so near to their
position that they could smell the burned gunpowder. The
NVA gunner had set up his camouflaged position at the
edge of the bamboo thicket. Barnett signaled to Arnason

that he wanted to silence the weapon, and Arnason shook his head vigorously in the negative; they were on a recon mission, and he wasn't about to give his position away by attacking a machine gun that had to be close to other NVA forces. Barnett frowned but obeyed his sergeant. The team slipped away from the thicket and had moved less than two hundred meters when the bamboo thicket erupted in a series of large artillery explosions. The machine gun had missed shooting down the Bird Dog, and the artillery observer aboard had called in a fire mission. Arnason was both happy and very angry. He was happy that the NVA gun had been destroyed, but what the fire mission had told him was the other units hadn't received his location, or they hadn't posted it on their maps. He had to move with even more caution, especially to keep from being observed from the air because the American observers would call in artillery on them if they were discovered.

Arnason found a good hiding place to spend the night by a shallow stream that was slow-moving enough not to create any noise. The team tried eating, but none of the men were very hungry. All of them had been living off pure adrenaline for the past thirty-six hours. They drank gallons of the cool, clear water during the night and listened to the NVA units passing near their position. Arnason risked calling back their location to the command post at LZ Mary and giving the captain information about the NVA troop movements and the direction in which they were traveling. Periodically during the night, artillery and mortar fire would shatter the stillness of the jungle plains.

The dawn of the second day brought a clearness in all of their senses. Woods noticed that his hearing had improved along with his sense of smell. He understood why Arnason insisted on living in a perimeter bunker away from congested troop billets.

Arnason tapped Sinclair's shoulder and then mimed with

his hand like he was putting on a hat and jacket. Sinclair nodded and opened up his pack. Barnett and Woods watched in astonishment as Sinclair slipped on an NVA tan jacket and pith helmet with a red star in the center. Arnason pointed down the path, and Sinclair took the point man's position. A surprise encounter with an enemy unit so far behind their lines would give the initial advantage to his team, and that's all he needed: an extra second to react.

Explosions filled the hot air all day long as the recon team traveled. Small-arms fire could be heard in the east for miles in every direction, along with rockets and artillery. The battle was still raging in the Ia Drang Valley. The team had reached the base of the Chu Pong Massif, and Arnason had slowed their pace down considerably. The NVA on the flat mountain would not be as alert as those in the valley, but they were as dangerous to a small recon team. Arnason had switched packs with Woods and rested during the break in carrying the heavy PRC-25 radio.

"Man! Oh, fuck me!"

The American voice stopped the breath in all of the team. It was totally unexpected.

"Keys. I'm fucking scared. . . ."

A sharp Vietnamese voice cut off the American, and the sound of something striking flesh could be heard.

Arnason dispersed his team and crawled forward toward the voices. He stopped short of an embankment and carefully parted the thick grass that edged a wide stream. Sitting on the far side were three American soldiers, two of them wearing 1st Cavalry shoulder patches, sitting under a thick clump of overhanging grass. A pair of NVA guards with fixed bayonets stood at each end of the group of POWs. One of the Americans was bleeding from his mouth. Arnason could see that his front teeth had been knocked out and blood poured from the wound. One of the

Vietnamese pointed up in the sky at a passing helicopter and spoke rapidly to his comrade.

Arnason felt a slight touch on his shoulder and looked over to see Barnett next to him. The young soldier's eyes gave away what he was thinking. Arnason nodded in the negative and slid back into the brush, tugging at Barnett's leg. There was a long pause, and the young soldier slid back down. They scurried back to Woods and Sinclair, who waited on guard twenty meters away.

Barnett crawled up to Arnason's ear and whispered, "We *must* rescue them!"

Arnason shook his head violently in the negative.

Barnett scowled and shook his head in the affirmative.

Arnason risked whispering. "We have a *mission*!"

"I don't give a fuck about the mission! I'm not going to let a bunch of gooks fuck with Americans!" Barnett almost broke out in normal conversation, and the quiet jungle seemed to echo his words farther than they actually traveled.

"No!" Arnason grabbed Barnett's collar and twisted.

"You and Sinclair and Woods . . . you go!" Barnett broke free. "But I'm going to get those guys or fucking die trying!" Barnett left the team without looking back. Arnason stopped Woods with his hand from joining his buddy.

Barnett slipped back to where they had been earlier and saw that the three American prisoners were still on the opposite side of the stream and that the two guards had sat down under the overhanging grass in the shade. It looked like they were waiting for something. Barnett didn't waste any time. He slipped his pack off his back, started a low crawl down the stream until he was out of sight from the NVA guards, and quickly changed sides for his crawl back. The first guard he saw had his eyes closed, but Barnett could tell by the way the man held his AK-47 that he was only resting his eyes and was not sleeping. Barnett felt his

heart smashing against his ribs as he closed the distance
between the two of them. One of the Americans shifted his
position just as Barnett slipped over the embankment and
shoved his K-Bar knife in the NVA's throat right below the
man's voice box. The NVA tried getting up on his feet, and
a loud hissing sound came from the hole in his throat. It
wasn't like he had seen in the movies. The man didn't die.
Barnett kneed the soldier in the groin and ran the knife
back into his chest. The NVA gasped and fell dead. Barnett
looked up, searching for the second NVA. One of the
Americans was staring at him in openmouthed shock at
seeing a camouflaged American holding a bloody knife.
When Barnett finally located the other guard, he saw that
the soldier was standing with his AK-47 pointed at him,
ready to fire. He knew that he was about to die.

Arnason watched the action from his concealed place on
the stream bank and knew that he had to do something
quick or Barnett was going to be killed. He dove from his
side of the stream bed using the edge of the embankment to
shove off from, holding his knife out in front of him. The
force from his wild push-off thrust the sergeant against the
NVA soldier, driving the sharp blade deep into the enemy
soldier's chest and knocking the squat man against the
nearest stunned POW. The barrel from the NVA's rifle
swung around and smacked Arnason alongside his
shoulder, and the round bayonet cut across his cheek. Arnason hit the gravel bed of the stream hard and saw stars
flash in front of his eyes.

Barnett recovered quickly and waved for the three
American POWs to follow him back across the narrow
stream to where Sinclair and Woods waited. The liberated
prisoners scurried up the muddy embankment without having to be told twice. Barnett paused and looked at the
dazed sergeant, who was on his hands and knees in the
stream shaking his head and trying to clear his vision. Bar-

nett went back and helped his recon team leader to his feet. He braced him up, and they both staggered over to the matted down spot on the bank. Barnett shoved his sergeant through the opening and looked both ways along the stream for any other NVA soldiers before he followed his leader.

One of the American POWs was shaking so hard from the fear and excitement over being rescued that he couldn't walk and dropped down on the matted grass. Woods grabbed him under one arm, and Sinclair lifted him under the other.

Arnason had regained his senses, tore open his backpack, and removed a regular mess-issue clear glass salt shaker that was filled with a white powder. Barnett looked at his sergeant, wondering if the experienced recon NCO had flipped out. Arnason pulled the small piece of green cloth tape off the top of the container and sprinkled the fine white powder all over the matted-down grass. He motioned for Barnett to catch up with the patrol and followed him, stopping frequently to powder their trail.

Arnason took the point after a few minutes and shot an azimuth with his compass for LZ Mary. He was not going to risk a heliborne extraction and have the pilots risk their lives. The area was controlled by the NVA. He had decided on walking out with the American POWs.

Night caught the team out in the open elephant grass, and Arnason formed a circular perimeter with his team. The three POWs collapsed, exhausted, in the center of the small circle and immediately fell asleep. Barnett caught Arnason glaring at him, and then the NCO smiled. He was pissed because Barnett didn't follow his orders but was very satisfied with the successful prisoner snatch.

The night was pitch-black; not even shadows appeared. The team relied totally on their sense of smell and hearing.

Woods knew that his team was all within a matter of a few meters from him, but in the dark he felt alone.

Right before first light, Barnett felt the hunger pains. He was starving after not having eaten in almost two days. He undid the ties on his backpack and reached inside for one of his prepared LRRP rations. A muffled cry reached him. He listened and heard it again. It was coming from one of the sleeping ex-POWs. Barnett slipped over to the man in the dark and felt him shaking. He ran his hand up his side until he reached the man's face and felt his cheeks. The POW had been crying in his sleep. Barnett ran his hand through the soldier's hair, trying to comfort him the best he could. It must have been pure hell being taken prisoner by the enemy. Barnett felt the man move in the total darkness and held the open LRRP ration against the soldier's chest. He felt the man take it and then heard him shoving the food into his mouth.

A bird singing woke Arnason. He had fallen asleep despite all of his attempts at staying awake. He rolled over and looked at his team. Everyone was sleeping. He stretched his leg and kicked Sinclair awake. Woods woke with a start; he had been dozing lightly. The whole team heard the dogs yelping in the distance. Arnason grinned; the powdered tear gas had worked.

Breakfast was a fast LRRP ration. Woods opened a packet of chili con carne and offered it to one of the ex-POWs. The man didn't hesitate taking the offered food and started wolfing it down using three fingers of his right hand for a spoon. Woods looked at Arnason, who had been watching; it was obvious the three ex-captives were starving. Arnason opened his pack and counted how many of the dehydrated rations he had left. He had only planned on two rations a day, and three days at the most in the field. It was lucky for the rescued men that the team had been too hyper to eat. Arnason had one packet of LRRPs that was already mixed with water, and he handed it to one of the men, who paused for a second with the green packet in his hand and then gave it to the third soldier. Arnason frowned and then shrugged his shoulders. He had no way of knowing that Barnett had given him a ration during the night.

The team crossed numerous trails in the sea of tall grass that were very wide and showed the passage of large units of NVA. Arnason paused frequently to listen. Visibility was less than five feet in the elephant grass, and their lives depended on their hearing. Woods and Barnett had given two of the ex-POWs their 9-mm pistols to carry in case they ran into a NVA patrol by accident, and Arnason loaned the third man his shotgun, which had been sawed off at both ends. The weapon was carried by Arnason in a special custom-made pouch on the side of his pack.

Arnason raised his arm slowly to stop his team. He had been traveling as the point man most of the patrol. It was too dangerous to train either Woods or Barnett, and Sinclair was the best tail-guard in the division. Barnett scrambled forward to join Arnason and to see what had stopped the team. Arnason pointed to the structure just a few feet ahead of him. The NVA had cut bamboo poles and had driven them into the ground, making a frame that had been covered with a coarse matting and had small bundles of elephant grass stuffed through it. The enemy lager site was perfectly camouflaged from the air and was large enough to hold a platoon of soldiers. Arnason could see used bandages piled up in one corner and a number of discarded medical supply boxes. They had stumbled on a forward hospital. Arnason placed his finger against his lips and listened for any sounds. A grass bird sang a vibrant song in the thicket, followed by an answering challenge from another male nearby. Arnason relaxed a little, knowing that the birds wouldn't be singing in that direction if the NVA were near. He used the opportunity to shoot another azimuth and selected a direction that he hoped would take them back to LZ Mary. Arnason didn't want to alarm the team, but he was lost, and had been lost in the tall grass for most of the patrol.

The recon team moved with extreme caution for the rest of the day. Woods could feel the slight rise under his feet and knew that they were climbing a gradual hill. Arnason felt the same pull against his legs and drew the team to the top of the rise. The elephant grass was much shorter on the top of the hill, and the team was forced to crawl. Arnason moved slowly, looking constantly for any sign of an enemy observation post. He broke through the grass and could see the river and the landing zone. Arnason couldn't help smiling. He had brought his team back by traveling in a huge circle. Woods crawled up next to the sergeant with the radio. Arnason was still smiling and keyed the handset twice and waited. There was no answer from the landing zone. Arnason signaled for the team to form a star defensive position on the swell in the ground and continued sending the two-click signal over the radio every five minutes.

The radio operator in the command post threw his open can of C-rations against the bunker wall. All of the men at LZ Mary were a bundle of raw nerves, and it took very little to set them off. They had been under enemy attack for ten straight days. "If that motherfucker doesn't stop keying his radio, I'm going to fucking scream!"

The captain looked up from the map where the forward observer from the artillery battery was plotting harassment and interdiction fires. He was selecting hilltops, ravines, and any heavy-growth areas that he could find on the map where the NVA could be hiding. "What did you say?" The captain went over to where the radio operator sat in front of the wall of radios. *"What did you say?"*

The man turned to look at his captain, knowing the pressure had forced the officer to go crazy. "Sir, some asshole is keying the radio and screwing up messages coming in from the companies."

The captain was about to answer when the static was broken by a keyed handset, returned, and was broken again. The captain waited for a third break in the static, but it didn't come. "That's our recon team! They're back!" He grabbed the handset and keyed it three times in rapid sequence. He waited a minute and repeated the process.

"Alert the perimeter that an American recon team is coming in!" The captain was excited; he had been sure that the team had been wiped out after not hearing from them in three days.

Arnason sighed when he heard the answering signal. "Let's go!"

The team had to hold themselves back from just running down the hill into the landing zone. Arnason moved even slower toward the friendly perimeter than he had moved through the elephant grass. He wasn't about to lose any of his team now that he was so close to safety. He tried staying close to the Ia Drang River and approaching the LZ from the water side of the base. The short three thousand meters took him almost five hours.

Their approach to the American perimeter surprised the guards, even though they had been alerted that a team was coming in. The base camp had expected them earlier. Arnason was the last one to enter through the barbed wire and meet the waiting captain.

"Who are these men?" The captain pointed at the three soldiers wearing tattered fatigues. One of the men wore a pair of jungle fatigue trousers that were little more than a rag wrapped around his waist.

"We found them." Arnason flinched at the loud sound of his own voice in a normal tone. "They were POWs."

"You rescued three POWs!" The captain's eyes widened. No one had ever rescued any American soldiers who had been taken prisoner by the NVA. "What unit are you men from?"

"From the 2nd Platoon, B Company, 1st Battalion, 7th Cavalry, sir—" The soldier's voice broke. "We were at LZ X-Ray and were taken prisoner when our platoon was overrun."

Arnason and his recon team listened as the soldier spoke. There hadn't been any conversation during the whole time they were on patrol, and they were hearing the man's story for the first time.

The soldier turned and faced Arnason. Tears rolled down the man's cheeks. "I don't know how to thank you."

"There's no need. You would have done the same for us." Arnason looked over at Barnett, who stood resting his CAR-15 on his hip and wearing a blank expression.

The soldier wiped his eyes with the back of his hands and continued. "They took us back into Cambodia as fast as they could, and I think they were keeping us in a holding area until they could bring all of the POWs together."

"There are more?" The captain was getting angry.

"We saw a group of five . . . maybe six," one of the other soldiers said.

"I've got to get you men back to division headquarters . . . immediately! Maybe we can send in a rescue team before our POWs are moved too far up north!" The captain picked up the handset and placed a call back to the division headquarters.

Arnason nodded for his team to leave the bunker and

assemble outside. He waited until all of his men were leaning against the shady side of the structure before speaking.
"You did good work out there, and I'm proud of you."

Sinclair nodded, Woods smiled, and Barnett looked back
out over the perimeter. He had loved every minute of it.

F O U R

Raw Meat

Staff Sergeant Arnason sat cross-legged on top of his fighting bunker. He had taken a long shower and changed into a clean set of fatigues. The sun was just beginning to set to the west, and the sky was filled with bands of beautiful colors. Arnason stared at the sunset and thought of home. He had been in Vietnam since December 1961— December 11, to be exact. He and Fitzpatrick had arrived in Vietnam with the 8th Transportation Company (Light Helicopter) from Fort Bragg, North Carolina.

Arnason lit a piece of C-4 explosive and watched the blue flame cover the putty-colored block. He set an open can of C-rations over the flame on his tiny homemade stove and waited for it to heat up. It had been over two years since he had eaten a meal cooked in a mess hall. The only prepared fresh food he would eat was French bread and cheese, which he would buy from the Vietnamese when the opportunity presented itself; he never went out of his way to find it. He picked up the wallet-sized picture of his two sons and daughter and looked at it in the soft light. He hadn't seen any of them in almost four years; the oldest boy would be fourteen now. Arnason rubbed the edge of the only snapshot he had of his family and thought of the good times he had with the kids before the divorce. He had loved his family more than life itself and had lost all of them when he divorced his wife. The judge thought that he was crazy during the divorce hearings, but the only problem was that he was too proud to tell the judge what had been occurring in his marriage, and his outburst in the courtroom had ended up with him spending thirty days in jail with his wife winning sole custody of the children. He had shipped out for Vietnam right after being released from the civilian jail and hadn't seen his family since.

"You're going to wear that picture out." The familiar voice of Fitzpatrick came from behind his right shoulder.

Arnason slipped the photograph back in the plastic protector and placed it in his right jacket pocket. He stirred his can of franks and beans and poured two teaspoons of Tabasco sauce over the steaming food.

"You want some company?" Fitzpatrick took a seat against the sandbag wall with his back to the perimeter. "I brought a bottle, just in case you might have changed your mind." He held up the fifth of Jim Beam.

Arnason still didn't answer. He tasted his beans and added another plastic spoon of red Tabasco.

"That shit will burn a hole through your guts!"

"What do you want, Fitz?" Arnason's voice reflected that his patience was growing short and he wanted to be left alone.

"That was a good mission you were on; the captain is putting in your whole team for a citation . . . you and that new kid, Barnett, for valor awards."

"I'm *impressed*, Fitz . . . and you should know by now, I don't give a fuck about medals." Arnason took a heaping spoonful of franks and beans in his mouth. He swallowed and then took a half dozen openmouthed breaths to cool down his burning tongue.

"Want a drink?"

Arnason shook his head. "This is just right!" He took another spoonful.

"What do you want in trade for Barnett?"

"I don't want to *trade* him."

"I'll give you any man in the platoon for him, plus a thousand dollars cash."

"I'll keep him."

"What's your problem? You queer for the kid?"

Arnason looked up over the edge of the camouflaged can and shoveled the rest of the food in his mouth before answering the platoon sergeant. "I'm going to let you live . . . only because I've known you since Fort Bragg."

"Get off that shit, Arnie! What's your fucking problem? You don't drink anymore . . . you live in this fucking bunker like a hermit! You don't even fuck anymore!" Fitzpatrick staggered to his feet. "When was the *last* time you've been laid?"

"I don't think that's any of your fucking business . . . *friend*!" Arnason looked up at his friend and then ran his hand over the blue flames of his cooking fire.

"You're not the only guy to get a divorce!" Fitzpatrick sat back down again, but this time he sat on the sandbag wall that faced the perimeter with his back exposed.

"I thought we were talking about me *selling* one of my men." Arnason spit out the word.

"I need a couple of good men. That guy James stays stoned all day and glares at me when I tell him to do anything." Fitzpatrick drank from the neck of the bottle. "I got in two more replacements. One of them plays a guitar all night and sings *Christian* songs, and the other one is a college dropout who stays stoned with James all day."

"You picked them."

"Come on, Arnie! I need *one* good recon man!"

"I don't *sell* my men. If Barnett wants to join your team on his own, I won't stop him." Arnason clipped short the end of his sentence, letting his platoon sergeant know that he was done talking about it.

"Good! I'll talk with Barnett, then." Fitzpatrick left the fighting bunker by walking down the slanted rear slope of stacked sandbags.

Arnason sat and listened to the sounds of the jungle coming from over the defensive barbed wire. He sat quietly for over an hour and watched the night fall over the ground.

"I ain't going no fucking where." The voice came from behind the sandbags in front of the fighting bunker. Barnett had been sitting there the whole time listening.

Arnason smiled.

The Brigade Recon Company commander was proud of the record his teams had set during the Battle of the Ia Drang Valley. The information the division had received from the teams had changed the course of the battle, and the North Vietnamese Army had ended up losing two of the three regiments they had committed to the fight. Staff Sergeant Arnason's team had brought back extremely important information concerning how the NVA was maneuvering in the valley that had changed artillery tactics and H&I fires. The three ex-POWs supplied information about the enemy supply routes in Cambodia that gave the Air Force a number of targets for special arc-light missions along the border.

"Where's Arnason?" the captain asked Sergeant Fitzpatrick.

"He's sick . . . got dysentery."

"Did he go to the hospital?"

"I don't know, but it's real bad."

"Well, I hate to have him miss his award ceremony." The recon commander looked back over his shoulder, hoping the sergeant would join the formation at the last minute.

The commanding general was personally presenting the recon-team awards. Barnett was receiving the Silver Star and a promotion, and Arnason was getting a Silver Star and a Purple Heart for the bayonet wound. The Purple Heart was the reason Arnason was faking being sick. He wasn't going to accept an award for a bayonet *scratch*!

Woods and Sinclair stood in formation and received their Bronze Star Medals with *V* devices for valor. The heat coming up from the hot PSP on the helipad that was being used as a parade field was beginning to make Woods sick. He could feel the soles of his boots heating up, making his feet burn. The awards formation consisted of almost a hundred men, four long ranks of twenty-five soldiers each. Woods couldn't figure out why most of the first two ranks were all officers. He hadn't seen that many of them in the field, and most of them were assigned to fire support bases.

"Corporal Spencer Barnett!" The division commander's voice calling out his friend's name brought Woods out of his daydreaming. "Front and center!"

Barnett hesitated, leaving the security of the mass formation and stepping out in front of the group of men. Woods nudged him and grinned that it was all right. The young seventeen-year-old left the formation and took up a position of attention directly in front of the major general. Barnett looked very small standing alone. He had just gotten a haircut, and during peak periods of hormone output he only needed to shave once a week. He looked like a high-school kid ready to receive an award from his school principal.

"I am proud to announce that Corporal Barnett's impact award has been approved for upgrading by the MACV

Commander." The general smiled, but the grin didn't look right on him. Barnett continued staring at a spot in space directly in front of him. The tall major general took the Distinguished Service Cross from his aide-de-camp and pinned it next to the Silver Star that was already on Barnett's left breast pocket. The general paused and then shook the teenager's hand. "I'd like for you to join me and my senior staff at mess tonight. Would you join us, Corporal?"

Barnett maintained his blank stare. "If my sergeant doesn't need me for duty, sir."

The aide almost started laughing at the young soldier's comment. The general had never invited an enlisted man to his table before, with the exception of the division sergeant major, who ate with him during the holidays.

"I think we can work something out, but please... check with your sergeant first!" The general returned Barnett's salute, and the recon man did an about-face and returned to his place in rank next to Woods. He noticed everyone staring at him, and then suddenly a group of grunts that had been watching the awards ceremony from the tops of the sandbag bunkers circling the helipad, began clapping and whistling their approval of Barnett's award.

One of the Air Cav troops started chanting, "Barnett... Barnett," and within seconds the whole area around the helipad echoed with his name. The general looked over at his aide and then at the first two ranks of officers who had just received awards for the Ia Drang fight; some of them justly deserved their decorations, but there was a large number who had exaggerated their "acts of valor." He saw the sheepish looks on the faces of those who were guilty. The general shook his head slightly; he tolerated the horribly one-sided awards system in Vietnam because it did raise the morale of the troops, especially when a young soldier like Barnett was recognized for outstanding action.

Sergeant Arnason could hear the troops cheering "Barnett . . . Barnett" from his fighting bunker. He stood in the shady doorway and looked in the direction of the helipad. It was obvious that Barnett's peers had approved of the high awards, and it was very rare that they would show it in such a manner. Arnason shook his head but kept the smile on his face; he was going to end up with a division hero on his hands.

The Battle of the Ia Drang had taken its toll of casualties, and the MACV Commander in Saigon gave the 1st Cavalry Division a month stand-down to reorganize and train their replacements. The recon company was full for the first time since it had been established, due mostly to the exceptional record they had earned during the battle.

Arnason had taken advantage of the break from combat to hone his team into a perfect fighting force. Fitzpatrick had stayed drunk most of the month, and James had spent his time preaching Black Panther doctrine to the new replacements and forming secret chapters of the militant organization in the division.

Sergeant First Class Shaw was happy with the constant flow of detail men to help him in the supply room. He had restocked his shelves from the division warehouses in Qui Nhon and had established a number of excellent black market contacts that were making him a very rich man. He had almost forgiven Arnason for standing up for the new replacements, but every time he saw Barnett or Woods with their CAR-15s, he got mad all over again. He had gone to the captain and had complained about the unauthorized weapons in the company, but after the Ia Drang, no one would dare trying to take Barnett's CAR-15 away from him. It was common knowledge that Barnett had eaten dinner with the division commander.

Woods picked the wrong time to enter the supply hootch.

Shaw looked up from his desk and saw him standing there. "What in the fuck do you want?"

"Our platoon sergeant sent us over here for the Qui Nhon detail." Woods ignored the crusty sergeant's belligerence and rolled his CAR-15 off his back so that the supply sergeant could see it and get even more pissed off.

"How many men did Fitzpatrick send?"

"Masters, Sinclair, Simpson, and myself." Woods nodded back outside where the rest of the platoon detail waited.

Shaw was happy. Simpson was the main drug dealer for the brigade, and he always paid a percentage when he used the supply detail as a cover for his drug pickup in Qui Nhon. "Get loaded up on the supply truck . . . and I don't want any dope smoking!"

"You don't have to worry about me, Sergeant!" Woods left the tent and boarded the deuce and a half without any canvas on the cab or the bed. A modified rack for an M-60 machine gun had been built over the shotgun rider's seat. Woods let Sinclair take the automatic weapon; he was reliable.

The 1st Cavalry had opened Highway 19 from An Khe to Qui Nhon for truck traffic during the daylight hours. A brave driver with an armored personnel carrier escort might risk the trip at night, but normally the traffic was restricted to daylight. The detail had planned on spending the night at the division supply area in the large complex at Qui Nhon, and Woods was looking forward to another steam bath. The week before, Spencer Barnett had actually spent an hour in one of the large resort-area steam baths and had returned to the base camp smiling.

There were a couple of areas along the road that were excellent ambush sites, but the main threat came from mines in the sections of the highway that were gravel. Navy Seabees were paving the highway all the way to

Du-Co, but the Vietcong were experts at deception and would even go so far as to cut out a section of the asphalt and place a mine under it. A fast-moving vehicle would never see the telltale lines in the road until it was too late. Twice the supply truck caught up to the engineer mine-sweeping detail and had to wait. Right before they reached the junction of Highways 19 and 68, they passed a three-quarter-ton truck on its side with the back wheels still spinning from the impact of hitting the antitank mine. The front half of the vehicle was gone. The small truck tried passing a column of M-48 tanks and had driven on the soft shoulder of the road. Sinclair turned on his seat and stared at the bloody windshield of the truck. A couple of tankers had gone over to help the injured occupants. Shaw waved his driver on; he wasn't going to waste any time on the road. The tankers could handle it.

Woods relaxed and laid his CAR-15 down across his legs when they reached the outskirts of the coastal city. A pair of MPs waved them through the barbed-wire barricade that signaled their official entry into the secured city complex. A danger still existed from 122-mm rocket attacks and an occasional Vietcong assassination, but for the most part the VC used the city as a free port and bought their supplies through it and had their families live there safe from American artillery fire.

Simpson hopped off the back of the truck as soon as they reached the shanty city that bordered the military supply complex. Shaw ignored the black soldier's exit. The cluster of plywood shacks housed the laborers who worked as maids and sandbag fillers for the base area. Prostitutes had built their small one-room shacks in the shanty city and made their livings off the soldiers who worked the ships, unloading their cargo, and off the field soldiers who came to the small port city to draw supplies. The presence of the prostitutes was always given away by the Eurasian children playing in the dirt streets of the shantytown.

Simpson darted down one of the narrow dirt streets and disappeared into one of the shacks. Two Vietnamese men were sitting inside; both of them wore tropical suits that were expensive. It was obvious that they didn't live there.

"Well, hello, my friend!" the smaller of the two Vietnamese said to Simpson in perfect English. "I was wondering if you were still in business."

"You can bet your yellow ass that this nigger is *always* going to be in business!" Simpson beckoned for the woman sitting in a corner of the dark shack to bring him a beer, and he missed the hateful look on the face of the second Vietnamese.

"Why do you call yourself nigger?" The Vietnamese frowned. "I thought that word was offensive to Negros."

"*Negro* is offensive to *black* people . . . and *I* can call *myself* a nigger, but no one else can." Simpson took a long drink from the cold beer the woman had taken out of the Styrofoam cooler. The block of ice had cost her more money than the beer had, but it was important that she was a good hostess to the drug dealers. She had survived the French occupation, and she knew how to play both sides of the fence. The two Vietnamese in her humble shanty were both members of the local Vietcong battalion and sold drugs to the Americans. The black soldier had been there before to buy cheap marijuana and heroin.

"What's the price for weed this week?" Simpson thought he knew the game. He had been a member of the Detroit drug gang called Young Boys Incorporated and had been given the choice of joining the Army or going to jail when he had gotten busted in a small raid. He had chosen the Army and had almost immediately started a drug operation. Simpson had just turned seventeen when the judge sent him into the military, and he had already accumulated over six hundred thousand dollars, which was deposited in the Detroit Manufacturer's Bank.

"For you, my friend, we always give a discount." The small Vietnamese grinned while his partner glared at Simpson. The larger man would enjoy killing the insulting black man.

"And the heroin?" Simpson pushed his luck as he always did with the pair of Vietnamese. "I want a twenty-percent discount. I give you a lot of business and I should have preferred-customer status!"

"Ten percent. We must make a profit too!"

"Fifteen!"

"Fine. You are too good of a customer to lose!" The smaller Vietnamese shook his head as if he were being cheated but had no control over it.

"Good! Twenty pounds of weed and a kilo of heroin . . ."

The smaller Vietnamese nodded at his partner, and the large man left the shack. The three remaining people in the building sat quietly waiting for the man to return. Simpson drank his second beer and smoked a cigarette. He wanted to laugh at the Vietnamese drug dealer but bit his lip instead; he was buying drugs from him at less than fifty percent of the cost back in the States, and the fool had just lowered the price another fifteen percent!

The Vietnamese sat waiting for his partner to return with the drugs, but his thoughts were on the orders he had received from his division commander earlier. He had been ordered to increase his drug sales to the American dealers working the units of the 1st Cavalry Division. There were many new replacements going to that division after the Battle of the Ia Drang, and the NVA wanted the new men drug-dependent. The fifteen percent reduction in price meant that he was selling to Simpson for less than it cost to produce and ship the drugs from Cambodia, but he *wasn't* a capitalist.

The large Vietnamese entered the shanty carrying a new U.S. Army duffel bag in one hand. Simpson took the olive-drab canvas bag, unsnapped the hook from the end, and looked inside. He saw the kilo of heroin on top of the one-pound clear plastic bags of marijuana.

"Looks good." Simpson reached into the side pocket of his jungle fatigues and removed a flat brown envelope. He opened it and counted out the price of the drugs with new American hundred-dollar bills. "Count it."

The small Vietnamese grinned. "I trust you, my friend." He stood and tucked the money away in his suit. "And when shall we see you again?"

"I'll try to make it on the next supply run." Simpson took the duffel bag and left the shack.

The large Vietnamese spoke in his native language. "I would *enjoy* killing that pig slowly!"

"Someday, my loyal friend, someday. . . ." The smaller Vietnamese patted his pocket. The green dollars would buy much-needed supplies for his battalion.

Simpson threw the duffel bag over his shoulder and walked through the gates of the American supply compound without being stopped. The MPs assumed that Simpson had gone to one of the shanty laundries and was bringing his clothes back to his hootch.

Shaw left the building as soon as he saw Simpson approach the truck. "Hey, buddy! We've got some business to attend to."

Simpson glared at the supply sergeant. He knew the man was taking him for a ride, but for the present he had to put up with him. "Yeah, business . . . is that what you call it?"

Shaw held his hands out, palms up, and shrugged his shoulders. "We *all* can get rich, partner."

"We ain't fuckin' partners!" Simpson increased the intensity of his glare.

"Come on...." Shaw led the way back to the storage shed he used for an office when he was in Qui Nhon. The senior NCO who ran the warehouse complex was an old friend of his from their days together teaching at the Quartermaster School in Fort Lee, Virginia.

Shaw took a seat on a bale of jungle boots. "How much are you bringing back?"

Simpson looked at his duffel bag. "Fifteen pounds of weed and a half-kilo of monkey."

"Really?" Shaw grinned. "Now let me see..." He opened the duffel bag and could see the kilo. "Simpson! This is a half K?"

"I meant a kilo."

"You're not trying to cheat a friend, are you?"

"I made a fuckin' mistake!"

"Let's tally your *transportation* costs. Twenty dollars a pound for the grass and a hundred dollars a kilo... that'll come to four hundred dollars."

Simpson reached into his side pocket, the opposite pocket from where he had paid off the Vietnamese, and removed a bundle of MPC ten-dollar notes. He counted out forty of them and handed the money to the sergeant. He had taken just about enough of the greedy NCO and was planning on paying James to give the white bastard a visit.

"No, no, my friend... *green* money, or make that twelve *hundred* dollars in MPC." Shaw hooded his eyes.

Simpson replaced the MPC and paid the sergeant in green money.

"Where do you get all of your *real* money from, Simpson?" Shaw tried pumping the black.

"*That* is none of your motherfucking business!" Simpson let the hate show on his face.

Shaw threw his head back and laughed. He didn't care where the money came from, just as long as it came to *him*.

Simpson picked up his cargo and left the building. He knew that in order to stay on Shaw's supply detail, he would have to continue paying the bastard off. Shaw was getting greedy, but without him Simpson would end up back on a recon team and risking his ass in the field. He was too rich for that kind of shit. Simpson smiled as he thought of the answer to Shaw's question. He had a *perfect* system of converting MPC to green dollars. He had started out by transferring a hundred thousand dollars from his Detroit account to a bank in Hawaii, and then he took an R and R to the islands and drew his money out in hundred-dollar bills. It was an easy matter of smuggling the money back into Vietnam from an R and R flight. He was making more money from converting MPC into green at a rate of three to one than he was selling drugs, but drugs was his *business,* and he would never give up his business. He was making so much money that his problem now was converting MPC. He had partially solved that problem through his addicts. He gave them free hits of heroin for personal checks made out to his accounts in Detroit and Hawaii. He would smuggle the checks out or have a brother take them back and deposit them in the accounts. The system was better than exchanging the money in Vietnam.

During the two years he had spent in Vietnam, Private Tousaint Simpson had become one of the richest men in the division.

Sergeant Shaw was up at first light. It was important to reach the docks before the supply of frozen meat ran out for the day. Large oceangoing refrigeration ships would lie off the beach out of mortar range and unload their cargo onto smaller LSDs that shuttled the food and equipment to shore. Shaw had already insured that his paperwork was in order for the brigade's order of frozen meat and for his *special* order that he had bought through his old school buddy for the black market at An Khe.

The detail waited on the truck for Shaw to clear the vehicle for entry on the docks. Woods noticed that Simpson had brought a duffel bag with him and had shoved it under the tarp, near the far corner of the steel truck bed. Woods knew that Simpson was a drug dealer and assumed that he had picked up his supply. It was none of his business, but staying alive was. Simpson could get a dozen addicts to frag him during the night or during the day, for a single free hit of the cheap drug.

Shaw left the security shack and waved the truck over to the loading dock. Four pallets of frozen meat waited for them under one of the roofed refrigerator areas. The meat had just come off one of the large ships and hadn't even been placed in cold storage yet.

"You guys are lucky!" Shaw yelled up to the detail. "I've found a forklift to load the pallets with."

Woods hopped off the truck and took a seat on the ground next to one of the large white portable freezers. He was joined by the rest of the detail as they waited for the truck to be loaded. Woods noticed that a convoy of trucks with Korean markings on their bumpers was parked in the line of freezers behind them. He was curious and walked over to where the yardmaster controlled the operation from his raised shack. The yardmaster could see all of the rows of freezers and the unloading operation from his ten-foot-high perch. The structure reminded Woods of a California lifeguard tower on the beach. Woods looked back and noticed that Masters had followed him.

"What's going on?" Masters caught up to Woods.

"There's a lot of Korean trucks in here. I was just curious . . ."

"Here comes Shaw. We'd better hide, or he'll chew our asses for coming over here!" Masters slipped behind a fence the yardmaster had built to keep the wind from blowing the sand away from the legs of his tower. Woods joined him.

Shaw climbed the ladder and entered the air-conditioned office. Woods and Masters could hear them talking through the cracks in the floor above them.

"Shaw! Good to see you again!"

"Yeah! Here's your money." There was a pause in the conversation while the yardmaster counted the stack of MPC.

"The price is going up ten dollars a case next week." The voice of the yardmaster sounded like gravel in a tin can.

"Again!" Shaw's voice filtered down between the planks. Woods was nervous; they were obviously hearing a conversation that wasn't meant for them to hear.

"It's not my fucking fault! The veterinarian has hiked up his fee to twenty grand a ship. He told the last captain that he wouldn't declare the meat unfit for human consumption unless he doubled his cut."

Shaw's voice leveled out. "Greedy! Every fucking body is getting greedy!"

"I know what you mean. We can all leave here million-aires if we *share*, but there's always the few that are going to fuck it up for all of us."

Woods smelled the acidic odor of a strong cigar and knew then why the yardmaster's voice sounded so bad.

"I've got to get my cargo back to An Khe before it thaws!" Shaw laughed. "No one wants to buy meat that's unfit for human consumption."

Woods elbowed Masters in his side and left the shelter of the fence. He ran bent over until they had cleared the row of freezers and were protected from being seen from the tower by staying close to the white containers that housed tons of meat and frozen vegetables intended for the American troops in II Corps.

When they were far enough away from the sergeants, Masters spoke. "Those black-marketing motherfuckers! Now I know why we don't have fresh meat in our mess halls and end up eating canned tuna three times a week!"

Woods remained silent.

"I'm going to turn those bastards in to the CID!" Masters was angry.

"Stay out of it, Masters. It ain't worth the trouble, and it's a bunch of sergeants and *officers* involved! You heard them talking about the veterinarian! Well, he's an *officer*!"

"Fuck them! I'm sick of eating shit while they're getting fucking rich!" Masters shook Woods's hand off his shoulder. "There's a CID office by the main supply complex. Tell that fucking Shaw to pick me up over there!"

"You're fucking up, Masters!" Woods tried again to talk the soldier out of reporting the incident. Low-ranking enlisted men never won when they went up against senior NCOs and officers.

"*You* stay the fuck out of this! I may be a fucking druggie, but I'm no fucking black marketeer!" Masters left Woods alone by the reefers and ran across the storage area toward the Criminal Investigation Division's office.

Woods yelled after him. "Don't get me fucking involved!"

Masters stopped running and called back. "Fine with me, you fucking coward!"

Sinclair and Simpson were just pulling the last heavy tarp over the pallets of frozen meat when Woods rejoined them.

"You timed it right, Woods!" Sinclair called down jokingly to his recon teammate. "We're done!"

"I'll unload." Woods pulled himself up on the truck.

"You bet your white ass you'll unload!" Simpson was mad. Simpson was always mad. "Where did you go?"

"To find a shitter." Woods made up the believable lie.

"Where's it at?" Sinclair asked. "I'd better go before we get out on the road."

"I couldn't find one back here, but I saw one behind the main office complex when we came in. Ask Shaw to stop when we leave."

"*Stop where?*" Shaw yelled up from the ground.

"Stop at the main gate so we can take a shit before heading on back." Sinclair took a seat against the cool stack of meat.

"I hope you strapped those pallets down good. If that meat shifts back there, it'll crush you." Shaw pulled himself up on the running board and slid over the passenger seat. "*Fuck!* This seat is hot!"

"Here." Woods threw him a piece of cardboard that had been used to make the pallets slide better on the bed of the truck during the loading. "Use this to sit on until the seat cools off."

"Where in the fuck is Masters?"

Woods dreaded the question.

"Probably hiding somewhere smoking a bowl." Sinclair leaned over the railing and honked the horn.

Shaw waited a few seconds and then told Sinclair to drive the truck to the main gate complex and they'd wait there while they used the latrine.

Masters had entered the CID office madder than when he had left Woods. He had taken only a few minutes to tell the CID sergeant who was on duty about the black marketing operation that was going on back in the refrigeration yard.

"Are you the only one who saw the two sergeants?" The voice of the CID man was soft.

Masters looked over at the sergeant, and was about to

mention Woods, then remembered that he didn't want to get involved. "Yeah . . . just me."

"Well, fill out this report form and I'll personally investigate the incident. I agree with you, we can't have black marketing going on here!" The sergeant handed Masters a preprinted form to fill out.

"Look, Sergeant Shaw is going to have to pass by here on his way out. Just check his paperwork and you'll see the difference in the amounts. . . ." Masters pointed back to where the truck had been parked.

"Thanks for your advice." The sergeant smiled politely. "But let me handle this . . . our way."

"Fine with me!" Masters shrugged his shoulders.

The screen door flew open, and Shaw strode into the office. "What the fuck are you doing in here?"

Masters looked up from the paper he was filling out. "Burning your ass, Sergeant!"

"What!" Shaw took an aggressive step toward the soldier.

"*Stop!*" The CID sergeant stepped between them. "I think you'd better be on your way, Sergeant!" The CID man shoved Shaw back toward the door. "Your man will be staying here with us for a couple of days, and we'll have him flown back to An Khe when we've finished with him."

"You motherfucker!" Shaw glared at the man. "Be careful what you say! You've got to come back to An Khe!"

"Fuck you!" Masters gave the departing sergeant the finger.

Shaw and Simpson were both worried over what Masters was telling the CID agent back at the supply compound as they drove through the city; neither one of them wanted to be investigated by the Army's special criminal unit, but most of all, they didn't want to lose their businesses.

Woods tried to keep a blank look on his face. He knew that either one of them—the drug dealer or the black marketer—could have him wasted. He couldn't figure out what motivated Masters to pull something so dumb. There was no way that Masters could return to the An Khe area after reporting the sergeant for black-marketing government supplies. Woods lost the blank look on his face and smiled; Masters had been looking for a way to get out of the field and find himself a desk job, and if Woods was right in his reasoning, Masters had found a way.

"Stop the truck!" Sinclair stood up behind Simpson, who had taken over driving back to An Khe. "Stop the fucking truck!"

"What for?" Shaw looked around nervously for Vietcong Sappers.

"Just stop the fucking truck for a second!" Sinclair grabbed his M16 and jumped over the railing to the sidewalk.

Woods watched him run across the street and over to a group of Vietnamese kids who were beating up a small boy. Sinclair pushed his way through the crowd and grabbed one of the Vietnamese kids by the hair and pulled him off the smaller boy. A pair of Vietnamese used the opportunity to deliver a series of kicks against the boy's body while he was still on the ground. A little girl, about seven years old, ran from the doorway in which her brother had shoved her for protection and tried punching one of the boys hitting her brother.

"*Di-di-mau!*" Sinclair growled at the gang of street urchins, and continued swatting at the dodging kids.

"Come on back here!" Shaw yelled from across the street. He was anxious to get back to An Khe and check with one of his buddies in the military police about Masters.

Woods noticed from his seat in the truck that the boy

Sinclair was helping had medium brown hair, not like the hair of the Vietnamese, which was always black.

Sinclair helped the boy to his feet and tried dusting off the adolescent's shirt. The ten-year-old twisted out of Sinclair's grip and ran a couple of steps toward the retreating gang before stopping and yelling after them in broken French that all of their mothers ate the sex organs of male water buffalo.

Sinclair caught the boy again and swung him around so that he could see him. "Do you speak English?"

The boy tried breaking free.

"Do you speak English?"

The little girl answered for her brother. "A little."

"What's going on?" Sinclair still spoke to the boy.

The ten-year-old stared at him for a couple of seconds before answering. "You like me!" He beckoned to his sister and spoke to her rapidly in Vietnamese. She stared at Sinclair.

"You part French . . . part Vietnamese?"

Sinclair understood. The two children were Eurasians; half French and half Vietnamese. Their father was probably some French soldier from the colonial days. "Where's your mother?" He looked around the street for the woman.

"Mother dead . . . VC . . ." The boy made a knife motion over his throat and gagged.

"Dead?" Sinclair had been around long enough to look out for a con job.

"Yeah, GI!"

"Where do you live?"

The boy looked puzzled.

"You sleep?" Sinclair pointed to the houses lining the street.

The street urchin shook his head in the universal sign for no. "I too young to fuck." The boy had mistaken Sinclair's question for a proposition.

"No!" Sinclair became angry, not at the boy but at the situation. "Hootch. Where's your hootch?"

"Here." The boy pointed to the street.

"Come!" Sinclair took the girl by the hand, then reached over and grabbed the ten-year-old. He had made a decision to take the children with them. If worse came to worst, the kids could live with one of the laborers who filled sandbags around the An Khe perimeter.

"What in the fuck are you doing with those kids?" Shaw leaned over the back of the truck bed and watched Sinclair hand the children up to Woods.

"I'm taking these kids with us back to An Khe, at least until next week's supply run." Sinclair wasn't asking permission, he was telling the sergeant. "We can bring them back when things cool off a little."

Shaw looked over at Simpson, who shrugged his shoulders and stuck out his lower lip. He could care less about a couple half-breed Vietnamese kids.

"All right! Fuck it!" Shaw slipped back down on his seat; he didn't want to get in a fight with Sinclair now. He had his own problems with Masters, and he figured Sinclair might come in handy as a witness. "But you take care of them, and if you get caught smuggling them into the base camp, I don't know a damn thing!"

The children hid under the tarp, between the pallets of frozen meat. It was the closest either of them had ever come to air-conditioning, and they liked the cool air that tickled their throats when they took a deep breath. The little girl giggled.

"You kids keep it quiet under there!" Sinclair said, hissing the words out between clenched teeth. They were passing through the base camp gates. The children didn't understand what he was saying, but his tone of voice told them to be quiet.

Woods waited until they were well past the MPs at the gate before asking Sinclair a question. "What are you going to do with them?"

Sinclair looked out over the hood of the truck. "I don't know . . . keep them here for a while. They can clean the hootches or polish boots—" A volley of artillery rounds being fired cut off his sentence.

Woods nodded. He was thinking about the supply trip. Who would believe him back home?

F I V E

Murder

Sergeant Arnason gave in and allowed the two Eurasian kids to stay in the fighting bunker with the team and Sinclair. The eight-man bunker had eight cots built into the sidewalls, and there were only four men on the team; besides, Sinclair wouldn't let the kids stay anywhere else. The kids worked hard for their keep; no one could say that they were freeloading off the Americans. The seven-year-old girl helped the company mess sergeant in the kitchen, and the boy worked in the hootches, cleaning up and shining boots.

A light knock echoed through the bunker. "Sergeant Arnason?" Lieutenant Reed stuck his head through the doorway.

"Yes, sir." Arnason continued cleaning the M-60 machine gun.

Reed stepped all the way into the bunker. "We've got to talk about those Vietnamese kids."

"So talk . . . sir." Arnason wiped down the tripod legs with a dry cloth and then set the M-60 back down on top of the stand.

"I don't think that it's a good idea letting those kids have the run of the place."

"You think they might be VC?" Arnason stood behind the machine gun and placed his right cheek against the cool black metal stock and checked the weapon's field of fire. He pushed the butt of the machine gun to the right, until he could see the white stake that marked his right-most final protective line, and then swung the weapon back to the left. The stake had been knocked down.

"It's not just that. It's having a little girl running around with all of the men." Reed started stuttering. "I—I mean, she just *walks* in the latrine without knocking . . ."

"Sir, she's *seven years old*." Arnason looked up at his platoon leader.

"But sometimes the men are naked."

"I'll tell the guys to be more careful in the future, but I don't think there's a soldier in the company who hasn't become attached to one of the kids." Arnason locked the traversing device on the M-60 and hung his arm over the butt of the weapon. "I mean, I've even seen *James* smiling at the girl."

"Don't you think someone might . . . ahhh . . ."

Arnason's voice dropped a dozen octaves. "That would be very *dumb*. If someone even tried messing with those kids, Sinclair would blow them away, and that goes for the rest of the company." The sergeant pointed over to a home-made sandbag and two-by-four chair. "Have a seat, Lieutenant. You and I have to talk for a bit."

The lieutenant hesitated and then took the offered seat.

"Let me tell you a little bit about Eurasian kids in Vietnam. First, they ain't allowed to attend school with the *normal* Vietnamese kids. Second, they ain't allowed to work in good jobs, like the rest of the Vietnamese kids. Third, they can't inherit land. Of course, with their fathers being French or American, what land can they inherit?

Fourth, they are harassed, beaten, laughed at, and ridiculed all of their lives because of their birth. Add to all of that the fact that their fathers were the *defeated* French, and the boys have no *honor*."

Lieutenant Reed nodded his head. He was beginning to understand why Sinclair wouldn't give up the kids.

"No, I don't think you quite understand . . . yet!" Arnason had just begun. "The girl *will* end up as a whore, and if we stay here a few more years, she'll be making a lot of money screwing American GIs for a Vietnamese pimp. The boy? God knows what'll happen to him! Now you want me to tell Sinclair—who, if you haven't noticed yet, is an Amerasian—you want me to tell Sinclair that he has to dump the kids back out on the street?"

Reed shook his head from side to side. "I . . . I wasn't thinking. I'll talk to the captain about letting them stay here as long as we're in An Khe."

Arnason smiled. "Why don't you try giving the kids a break yourself, sir? They're really just like kids back home."

Reed paused in the doorway and looked back inside. "I can't promise anything."

"I know, sir. Just do your best." Arnason slowly blinked his eyes.

Lieutenant Reed hadn't been gone from the bunker for more than a minute when Sinclair burst through the entrance. "What did he want, Sarge?" Reggie was out of breath from his run across the company area. He had seen the lieutenant enter their bunker and suspected trouble.

"He wanted to talk about the kids."

"About what?"

"That really doesn't matter." Arnason stacked two green ammo boxes on top of each other. "What matters is he's going to talk to the captain about keeping the kids here as company mascots."

"Shit! That's great!"

"I thought you'd like it." Arnason grinned. "Now find Woods and Barnett, then check the barbed wire in front of our bunker and check the claymores . . . the wires too!"

"Yes, sir!"

"Dammit! Don't call me *sir*. I *work* for a fuckin' living!"

"Yes, *Sergeant*!"

Simpson sat around the wooden spool they used for a table with Brown, Kirkpatrick, and James. The conversation was drugs.

"I want to increase our sales to the artillery units." Simpson pointed with his long fingernail in the direction of the artillery batteries. "They aren't buying anywhere as much as they should be."

"Maybe we've got some competition springing up down there." Kirkpatrick had been given the quadrant of the An Khe base area that housed two infantry battalions and the artillery battalion headquarters.

"There ain't no *GI* competition for us on this base!" Simpson rapped out the sentence. "We run it all! Now, there may be some nickel and dime shit coming in from the ho's outside the gate, but that's nothing! I told you before: Be *reliable* and they'll buy from you. Why? 'Cause they're scared shitless that the VC will spike their dope with poison!"

"Enough!" James stood up. "Where's the fuckin' money you promised for our Panther chapter back home? I got a letter from them and they ain't seen shit!"

"Relax, bro! I said I'd mail them a check . . . and I will!" Simpson waved James back down in his seat.

"You damn sure had better! I haven't agreed to be your enforcer for fuckin' nothing!" James shook his fist. "Send the check! Fifty thousand!"

Simpson nodded in agreement and signaled that the

meeting had ended. Kirkpatrick and Brown left the bunker together and headed over to the mess hall for supper.

"I don't know about that James guy, bro," Brown said to his hometown buddy. "He's crazy."

"Yeah, I don't think it was such a good idea getting involved in this drug-dealing shit." Kirkpatrick knew his feet were getting cold. He enjoyed turning a buck like anyone would who came from New York, but he didn't like the smell of things.

"For *once* I agree with you." Brown squeezed Kirkpatrick's shoulder. "When we go back to the field, I'm telling Simpson that we're out of it."

"Good! I'd rather hustle supplies. No one gets hurt doing that but Uncle Sam!" Kirkpatrick started strutting sideways down the path. "Sergeant Shaw ... my main man!" He waved over at the sergeant, who had just left his tent.

The Criminal Investigation Division agent looked out over the small bay that had seven ships waiting to unload their cargoes. The harbor was a busy little port, not as large as ports such as Cam Ranh Bay, Nha Trang, Da Nang, and the largest one of all, Saigon, but fifty or sixty ships a month unloaded there.

"What are we waiting for?" Masters sat in the chair across from the CID agent and smoked a cigarette.

"I've got help coming from downtown, and when he arrives, we're going to go out to the refrigerator ship that unloaded this morning and check their paperwork. If what you're saying is true, I want evidence before I approach the chief veterinarian with charges against his people."

Masters nodded his head in agreement; what the special agent said made sense. The screen door to the small office squeaked open and closed, and a voice called out to the CID man, who answered from his office to come in. Masters looked up and saw the middle-aged NCO, wearing master sergeant stripes, smiling from the doorway.

"Are you ready?" The CID agent left his desk.

The master sergeant smiled and nodded his head.

"Good! Let's get this over with. I've got to get over to the club tonight for a no-limit poker game with some Navy types!" The agent led the way out of the office over to the harbormaster's speedboat. The master sergeant helped untie the boat from its moorings and pushed it away from the pier.

Masters took a seat in the center of the speedboat and braced himself as the nose of the craft lifted up off the water and the boat gained speed. The agent made a wide arc in the bay and then headed out to the ship that was located farthest out to sea. After a couple of minutes he lowered the speed, and the nose of the craft dropped back down in the water. The boat was almost at an idle.

"Are you sure you were alone this afternoon?" The agent smiled. "We sure could use another person to testify. You know, two are a lot better than one."

Masters became angry. He would like to bring Woods into it, but he had promised to leave him out of it. "Look when we get out there to the ship. You'll see that I'm not bullshitting! If you would have stopped Sergeant Shaw's truck, we wouldn't even have had to come out here!"

The agent kept smiling.

"You should have minded your own business, boy." The voice sounded like gravel in a tin can.

Masters felt the arm wrap around him and grab his chin. He elbowed the master sergeant hard in the chest, but it was too late. The sharp knife cut through his throat and windpipe and hung up against his spinal column. Masters felt someone pushing him overboard, and then the salt water entered his cut throat, and he felt the burning sensation. Masters knew that he was dying, and he also realized that there was nothing he could do about it. He just hoped that he would be dead before the sharks came.

The CID agent reversed the engine in order to dock the boat. He hadn't spoken a word to the yardmaster since leaving Masters floating in the harbor. He knew that by morning there wouldn't be anything left of the soldier. A resident population of sharks lived in the bay and fed off the spoiled meat that was thrown overboard from the ships. A cold shiver traversed the agent's spine as he recalled the first time he had witnessed a feeding frenzy. He had gone out to one of the freezer ships with the veterinarian to observe the destruction of two hundred and fifty cases of meat that had spoiled during the transoceanic voyage. The medical officer had signed the paperwork for *five* hundred cases of meat that was unfit for human consumption; he had discovered the minor error and had been invited into the business. The veterinarian had broken the seal on the freezer door, and the smell of rotting flesh rolled out over the deck. He had almost vomited then, but it wasn't until they started throwing the rotting meat overboard and the hundreds of small sharks began tearing at the heavy cardboard cases that he lost his breakfast. He had a very good imagination for a CID agent.

The yardmaster tied the boat to the mooring and started walking away from the dock.

The CID agent called after the NCO. "You have a long talk with Shaw! He damn near fucked up this operation!"

The yardmaster kept walking; he didn't have anything to say.

The agent tried avoiding the open water of the bay, but his eyes brushed over the calm water and locked in on the silhouette of the distant ship. He felt his hands start to shake and then his stomach roll. It was the thought of all of those *small* sharks tearing at the young soldier's body, taking baseball-sized bites out of him. The agent threw up all over the dock. He had a good imagination.

Corporal Barnett and Sinclair had the ten-to-two late-night watch on the perimeter. The graveyard shift was the most hated by the soldiers because it screwed up their whole night's sleep. Barnett didn't care about the shift back in the base area because the following day didn't require humping in the jungle.

A hand flare popped and floated down over the perimeter wire from a bunker farther down the line. Barnett used the soft light to check between the rows of barbed wire for Sappers. An Khe was a large enough base camp to be fairly secure from a major enemy attack, but Vietcong and NVA Sappers were very good at slipping into a base area and blowing up a couple of supply bunkers or ammunition dumps. The threat was a real one but wasn't taken seriously by most of the rear-area troops. Barnett took everything seriously and was quickly becoming a replica of Arnason.

"See anything?" Sinclair whispered softly, even though the perimeter bunkers were saturated with sound coming from inside the base camp.

Barnett shook his head and leaned back against the soft sandbags.

A small head popped up in the dark hole that occupied the center of the bunker roof. "What are you doing up this late, Trung?" The little girl hurried over to Sinclair and cuddled up against his chest. He was sitting on the bunker roof with his legs stretched out and crossed on the sandbags. The little girl straddled his legs and laid her head against his chest. Sinclair wrapped his poncho liner over the child, and within seconds she was sleeping soundly again.

"It must've been a bad dream." Barnett pointed back at

the roof exit. "You've got more company." He smiled in the dark. Jean-Paul moved slowly, half asleep, and found Sinclair. He slid up next to the soldier and reached under the liner until he could touch his sister before falling asleep, leaning against the man.

"I hope we don't get attacked tonight!" Barnett shook his head. "You wouldn't be much good!"

"Yeah." Sinclair was enjoying the love that was coming from the sleeping children.

A machine gun firing broke the stillness of the late night. Barnett and Sinclair looked in the direction from which the tracers were flying through the air. One of the guards was either jumpy or bored. A single 105-mm howitzer fired an H&I round out into the dark jungle.

"What are you going to do with them when we leave here?" Barnett left his seat and slid closer to Sinclair so they could talk softly.

"I don't know. I wrote my dad and told him about Trung and Jean-Paul." Sinclair placed his hands under the girl's small rear end and pushed her up higher on his chest so that he could breathe better. "Dad's a good man and has been in the Army for twenty-six years. He should be able to find out if I can ship them back to the States."

"You're going to raise them?" Barnett was surprised. Sinclair was only two years older than himself.

"I'll be responsible, but I've got some good parents; they'll help out." Sinclair's voice lowered. "I know that I can't leave them here."

"Can't you find a good orphanage for them?"

Sinclair turned a little so that he could see Barnett. "Man, you don't understand how they treat half-breeds in Asia! Blacks think they have it bad in the States! Shit! You haven't seen prejudice until you've been around these Orientals! I mean, they hate Oriental mixes like half-Korean and half-Chinese. You've got to be *pure* or you're nothing at all. I think it's because there's so much competition because of overpopulation that they won't accept anything that's flawed, and half-breeds are flawed!"

"I didn't think about that."

"Well, believe me, these kids have *nothing* to look forward to living here." Sinclair's jaws tightened, but Spencer couldn't see the anger in the dark. "You'd think their father or fathers would have known better than to have left them over here after they went back to France!"

"You probably have a better understanding about it than most people." Barnett stood up and walked over to the edge of the bunker and looked down to check close in.

"Yeah, I'm Amerasian, but if we'd stayed in Korea, my mother would have been treated very badly and my life would have been pure shit."

"Your dad's a career man?"

"Yes, and so was his father. They go all the way back to the Civil War."

"What's his rank?"

"Colonel. He hopes to be on the brigadier general list this year."

"Hot shit!" Barnett thought his father was a sergeant.

"He works hard at being the best." Sinclair felt Trung wiggle and tried adjusting her legs to make her more comfortable. "He wanted me to go to West Point, but I felt I should serve in the war first. In four years it will be over and I'd have missed it."

"Yeah, I can understand that." Barnett threw his poncho liner over his weapon. He could feel the early-morning dew rolling in to leave a light coat of moisture on everything.

"I have my application in already through the enlisted program, and as soon as my tour is up here, I'll go."

"A West Pointer!" Barnett was teasing his fellow soldier.

"You should think about going."

"Me?" Barnett chuckled. "I'm from *poor* people. Shit, man, I've spent my whole life in foster homes and the juve!"

"The Army doesn't care. The enlisted West Point program judges you on what *you're* worth, and not your parents or how much political pull your dad has." Sinclair's voice was serious. "You're undervaluing yourself. I don't think you realize, Spencer, you're one of the most decorated men in the division, *and* even though you act dumb, you're smart!"

"Who says I act dumb!" Barnett was joking with Sinclair. He knew what he had meant.

"I'm not talking *book* smarts. We all know you've got your shit together in one tight bundle in the field, and you can't be *dumb* and make it out there."

"I'll talk to Sergeant Arnason about it. West Point?" Barnett was beginning to like the idea.

"If you decide to try, I can help you with the paperwork, and my dad knows everyone in the Pentagon who can help—"

"Hold it! If I decide to go, I want to make it on my own!"

"Hey, asshole! I'm not talking about pulling strings to get someone in who's not qualified, I'm talking about *friends* helping to speed up the process!"

"Oh."

Trung wiggled and opened her eyes. She whispered in Sinclair's ear.

"She has to go to the bathroom . . . just great!" Sinclair shook Jean-Paul gently to wake him up. "Jean-Paul? Would you take your sister over to the latrine?"

The boy nodded, half asleep.

"Wake up." Sinclair smiled and wiped the boy's eyes, gently using his thumbs. "I don't want you wandering into the barbed wire."

Jean-Paul took his sister's hand and led her toward the nearest latrine, fifty meters away near the tin-and-plywood barracks. The moon had come up and was giving off enough light to see by.

Spencer twisted open his canteen and took a long sip of the lukewarm water to lubricate his dry throat. "Do you really think I could make it to West Point?"

"I wouldn't have mentioned it if I didn't think so." Sinclair looked at the face of his watch. "It's ten minutes till two, time to wake up Woods and Sarge."

"I'll do it, you watch the kids." Barnett dropped down into the dark interior of the fighting bunker.

Sinclair sat on the edge of the sandbags and watched for the children. They had been gone long enough and should be leaving the latrine. He squinted his eyes to see better in the partial light and looked off-center for their shapes on the path. They weren't there, and he started wondering if Trung was sick; both of the kids suffered from frequent diarrhea. Jean-Paul had a tapeworm when he first arrived, and the company medic now had the twenty-foot-long white worm in a glass jar on his desk.

The series of rapid, soft pops drew Sinclair's attention back to the perimeter. He caught the quick flash of what looked like shooting stars in the sky and realized shooting stars rarely appeared a dozen at a time. He recognized the threat and yelled out loud, "*Rockets*! *Incoming rockets*!"

Barnett poked his head out of the roof opening.

"*Get back down there*!" Sinclair used his boot to push Barnett back inside, and then he remembered the children.

Sinclair rushed to the side of the bunker and screamed. "*Trung*! *Jean-Paul*! *Get in a bunker*!"

The rockets landed in the base area almost in unison; over fifty explosions shattered the quiet of the night. Men began yelling to each other and running around in all stages of undress carrying rifles. The artillery started firing counter-battery fires, and the perimeter opened fire to clear the barbed wire of any Sappers who might be following up the rockets. Mortars that had been placed around the perimeter began firing illumination rounds, and the whole An Khe base area became an instant war arena.

Sinclair could see clearly all the way back to the barracks but couldn't locate the children. He saw the latrine and it was still intact. The sound of helicopters warming up and taking off filled the night sky. One after another of the gunships peeled off their helipads and flew to their assigned sectors to search for the enemy positions and also to protect the Hueys from additional damage in case the Vietcong decided to follow up the rocket attack with a ground assault. The sky was filled with blinking lights and roaring choppers. It looked to Sinclair like a hornet's nest that had been disturbed.

Arnason and Barnett came up through the roof. Woods remained inside to man the M-60 in case of a ground attack.

"What's going on?" Arnason listened as Sinclair briefed him on where the rockets had come from, and then used the land line to call the information back to brigade headquarters. Arnason had just hung up the telephone when he saw Trung and Jean-Paul leave one of the personnel bunkers behind the troop billets and start running toward the perimeter bunker. He grabbed Sinclair by the shoulder and pointed at the kids.

Sinclair went over to the edge of the bunker smiling; they had used their heads and had found shelter during the attack. He waved for the kids to run faster, and they obeyed. The flares being dropped by an Air Force flare ship lit up the area better than daylight.

Sinclair heard the sound at the same time Arnason saw the telltale flashes in the distance. He waved with both arms to the running kids. "*Get back! Get back!*"

It was too late. The second volley of rockets detonated on impact.

The ear-shattering explosion knocked Sinclair flat on his back, and Arnason was pushed down against an ammo box that cracked two of his ribs.

Trung's screams were the only thing Sinclair could hear above the roar of gunfire and counter rocket explosions from the attacking gunships on the exposed VC positions. The second volley had been both smart and dumb on the part of the VC; no one had been expecting the second volley at the base area, and if the VC would have set the second volley off by remote, then they would have survived the attacking gunships.

Sinclair struggled to his feet and jumped over the sandbags lining the fighting bunker. He ran toward the little girl's screams and found her sitting next to her brother. A foot-long gash exposed Jean-Paul's right lung and ribs.

Sinclair heard his own voice screaming, "*Medic! Medic!*" He could see the exposed lung moving in and out and realized that the boy was still alive. He comforted the crying girl and watched the medical team work on the boy.

Arnason watched from the bunker. He could spare Sinclair, but the rest of the team had to stay and defend the perimeter in case of an attack.

Sinclair followed the stretcher bearers to the medical station with Trung, who refused to leave her brother.

"He dead?" Barnett's voice was a whisper.

"I don't know. I couldn't see from here." Arnason blinked. "I hope not. Sinclair will be a basket case."

"So will I." Barnett didn't hold back his feelings.

The doctor had started working on the boy as soon as he reached the blacked-out surgical bunker. There were a half dozen injured men on the cots in the outer room, but none of them had been hurt seriously, and medics were dressing their wounds. Most of the injuries were from pieces of flying debris because the men had been sleeping in prone positions.

Sinclair and Trung waited while the doctors worked on the boy to stabilize his condition before having him flown to a hospital on the coast.

A large fighting bunker a hundred meters down from Arnason's opened fire with their .50-calibers and the two M-60s that were mounted inside. A squad of NVA Sappers tried escaping from the intense barrage and were cut to pieces. Arnason and Barnett dropped down inside of the bunker and scanned the area in front of their bunker for any of the enemy elite infiltrators. The barbed wire in front of them was clear. A number of claymores were detonated to the right side of Arnason's bunker, and the chatter of small arms followed. It seemed as though the NVA knew better than to try to infiltrate past Arnason and Barnett's fighting position. The lack of activity made Barnett nervous.

Sinclair stood when he saw the doctor approaching; blood covered the front of the surgeon's light green gown, and a portion of the mask he had hanging around his neck had a bright red spot of blood on it.

"Did you bring the boy here?"

"Yes, sir."

"He's stable for now. I'm having him shipped to the ARVN Hospital in Pleiku." The doctor turned to leave.

"Sir, you can't do that!"

"Why not?" The anger in the doctor's voice came from a mixture of fear that was normal during an attack, and from the soldier questioning his decision.

"He'll die in an ARVN hospital! Can't you see he's a half-breed!" Sinclair took a step toward the doctor. "Send him to our hospital in Qui Nhon."

"I can't do that. He's Vietnamese, and he has to go to a Vietnamese facility!" The doctor left Sinclair and the girl in the entrance of the bunker and returned to his operating table.

Sinclair grabbed Trung by her hand, and in the confusion he removed one of the M16s from the weapons rack by the door. The medical evacuation helipad with the large white circle and red cross painted on it was located near the rear entrance of the medical bunker. A couple of walking wounded were waiting to load up on an arriving MEDE-VAC helicopter. Sinclair took up a position near them and waited for the chopper to land. He could see Jean-Paul on a stretcher just inside the bunker. He had been placed there with an IV in his arm, waiting for an ARVN chopper to come and pick him up.

Sinclair tapped one of the wounded men on his shoulder and pointed to the stretcher with the boy on it. "Can you help me load him up?"

The slightly wounded soldier nodded his head and grabbed one end of the stretcher while Sinclair took the other. They slid the boy on the American MEDEVAC, along with the other American wounded. Sinclair lifted Trung up beside her brother and then hopped on the aircraft behind the pilot. He waved for the ship to lift off. The pilot gave him the thumbs-up sign, and the chopper banked away, headed toward Qui Nhon.

The surgeon stepped out from the bunker waving his hand at the chopper; he was a couple of seconds too late.

Sinclair comforted Trung and held Jean-Paul's hand during the short flight to the large American hospital. Medics and nurses were waiting on the helipad for the arriving wounded and immediately began separating the serious cases from the walking wounded. One of the nurses rushed over to the boy's stretcher and started issuing orders to the medics. She read the tag attached to the boy and called out, "Take him into surgery. He's been prepped already, and he needs a lung-and-heart surgeon fast!" She looked over and saw Trung holding Sinclair and quickly put the whole picture together; she had been in Vietnam for two straight years and knew instantly what was going on. "Soldier! Take the girl and wait for me in the main reception area! *Move!*"

Sinclair obeyed.

Arnason and his team left the bunker and watched as the gunships made passes at the jungle surrounding the base camp. It was almost noon, and the mopping-up action was still going on. A battalion from the brigade had been flown back from the field to sweep the area. Forty-six dead NVA Sappers had been found in the barbed wire at different locations around the base camp, and a small number of the NVA unit was trapped in the hills to the east of An Khe.

"They sure waste a lot of ammo." Woods shook his head.

"It keeps them fucking busy . . . and off our asses." Arnason opened a breakfast can of C-rations. He hadn't eaten since the night before and felt like having eggs and ham.

"Who, the NVA?" Barnett frowned.

"Naw, the *brass*."

Woods pointed out over the open area behind the bunker to a cluster of buildings. "Here comes the lieutenant."

"Shit!" Arnason set his can of food down on one of the sandbags and looked over toward the medical bunker. "If he asks about Sinclair, I'm going to tell him that I sent him back to supply to get some hand grenades."

The lieutenant approached the bunker wearing a grin on his face. The officer's cheeks were tinged with red from the excitement of the early-morning attack. "How are you men doing, Sergeant?"

"Fine, Lieutenant, just fine." Arnason answered for the group.

"Lots of action this morning!" The lieutenant was still

suffering from the excitement of the rocket attack. "One of those 122-mm rockets landed in the hootch next to mine!"

"Really?" Arnason tried not to show his lack of concern.

"Those damn things are bigger than an artillery round!"

"Yes, they're the size of the soviet 122-mm howitzers . . . and they do make a big bang!" Arnason tried smiling at the junior officer. "Now you know how Charlie feels when we drop artillery in on him."

"There were nine killed up at brigade headquarters. We had a couple of wounded but no serious injuries." The officer climbed on top of the bunker and looked out over the perimeter fence. "Nothing happened here?"

"No, sir . . . on both sides of us but nothing here."

"Oh." The lieutenant sounded disappointed. "What's that down there in the wire?" He pointed with his finger.

"A couple of dead Sappers." Arnason acted nonchalant.

"Sappers?"

"Yep, dead ones."

"I think I'll go down there and check it out." The lieutenant started leaving the bunker and paused. "Oh, by the way, we got a radio message in last night from Qui Nhon. Private First Class Daryl Masters was killed by the VC last night."

"By the VC?" Woods said from his seat on the sandbags. "He was in the supply complex."

"Yes." The lieutenant glanced over at Woods. "The VC seem to be able to go anywhere in this damn country!"

"But, sir! He was with the CID when we left him." Woods was having a hard time believing the Vietcong could infiltrate the major complex and kill soldiers.

"What has that got to do with it?" The lieutenant wanted to go look at the dead VC, and Woods was keeping him from it.

"The CID office is by the docks, way inside the perimeter."

"Who says that he didn't go downtown?"

"Where did they find his body?" Woods was very curious. Arnason listened to the conversation. He sensed Woods knew something about Masters that he wasn't sharing with the officer.

The lieutenant started walking away from the bunker but paused long enough to answer Woods's question. "He was found on the beach with his throat cut. Sharks had eaten half of his body. They think a whore might have done it." The lieutenant left the bunker.

"But, sir!" Woods started after him.

"Let him go." Arnason caught Woods by his shoulder. "He would rather look at dead VC."

Sinclair sat with his back against the wall and dozed off in an exhausted sleep, jerking awake whenever he heard someone approaching. Trung had fallen asleep in his lap.

"Soldier?"

The voice woke Sinclair, and he struggled to get on his feet.

"Soldier, relax." It was the nurse who had told him to wait in the reception area. "He's doing fine." She smiled. "Just fine."

"Oh, man!" Sinclair felt the tears well up in his eyes and blinked hard to keep them there.

"He's going to have to stay in a hospital for a couple of weeks. We'll transfer him to the ARVN hospital as soon as he can be moved."

"No!" Sinclair set his jaw. "You can't do that!"

"He's Vietnamese. He has to go there."

"No, he's not! He's my . . . he's my *son!*" Sinclair blurted out the words.

The nurse looked at the small girl he was holding. "And I suppose she's your daughter too?"

"Yes. Yes, she is. . . ."

The nurse looked at Sinclair and almost started laughing; she could see the soldier wasn't older than nineteen, maybe twenty at the oldest. "You started having a family awfully *young*, didn't you?"

"Yes. I was over here with my family. My dad is a colonel, and he was with a MAAG mission."

"I'd say you must've been *ten*...maybe *eleven* years old?" She couldn't help grinning at the attempt.

"Yeah. Us Orientals mature early." Sinclair realized he was making a fool out of himself.

"Well, I'll tell you what. The boy is going to need some good therapy when he comes out of post-op. It might be good if he saw his sister."

"Thanks!"

"And seeing that they are *Americans*, he can stay in our hospital, but only until we check his birth certificate."

Sinclair's face dropped.

"That should take a month or so." She smiled. "And I'll tell you what, young man: I've got a big room in the BOQ nurses quarters, and the girl can stay with me until the boy is ready to get discharged. How's that?"

"Oh, ma'am, thanks! You really are a lifesaver! I've got to get back to my unit or—"

"I figured that much out on my own." She wrote down her name and address on a card and handed it to Sinclair. "Here's where to contact me."

"I owe you a lot."

"You could write down *your* name and unit so I can find you, and you could tell me a little about *your* kids...like their names?"

Sinclair laughed and briefed the nurse on what was really going on. She listened intently, and when he had finished, she spoke again. "I liked your original story better. You being their *father*. Once you leave here, no one will know how young you are, and they won't *dare* ship the kids out knowing that they're Americans. Being Eurasians makes it even easier to believe. . . ."

"Believe me, this is the first time in their lives that being a Eurasian has been something *good*."

S I X

The A Shau
Reconnaissance

She was in constant pain and had been ever since she had mated with the smaller male the month before. He'd had a very difficult time mounting her because of the injury to her hip that had been caused by the bomb blast two years earlier. The male had been persistent and had bred frequently with her during her first season. She had mauled him so badly during their lovemaking that he had died a week later, and she had fed off his carcass for three days before she left their love nest and followed the sounds of the explosions for her next meals.

Lieutenant Reed sat in front of the large briefing map with Fitzpatrick and Arnason and watched the captain's wooden pointer tap the battle map almost where the South Vietnam border touched Laos and North Vietnam.

"The 5th Special Forces Group has an A-team working out of the A Shau . . . here." He went up close to the map, located the camp, and then stepped back and tapped the overlay. "In Thua Thien province. The A-camp's mission is border surveillance and the interdiction of NVA infiltration routes into South Vietnam from the Ho Chi Minh Trail that the NVA are building along the borders of Laos and Cambodia...here." The recon company commander tapped the map along the suspected route for the trail.

Fitzpatrick glanced over at Arnason; they both knew that if the North Vietnamese Army was building a main infiltration route to the south, it would be guarded by a large force of regulars.

The captain was looking at Fitzpatrick when the sergeant returned his attention back to the map. He had read the NCO's mind. "Your mission will *not* concern the trail across the border. That is directly..."

Arnason thought, Here comes the hook.

"You're going to be inserting seismic intrusion devices."

"What?" Fitzpatrick scowled.

The captain walked over to a field table that had been set up near the map and lifted up a device that looked like a land mine with a bamboo shoot attached to the top of it. "This is a new piece of equipment that has been designed to monitor enemy movement through ground vibrations."

Arnason became very interested and leaned forward in his seat.

"Your mission is going to be to bury these devices along selected trails in the mountains to the west of the A Shau Special Forces Camp." The captain looked up at the group of recon leaders. "Come over here so that you can see." He used the sensor to wave them over to the table. "These devices go in the ground up to here...." He showed with his fingers about an inch of dirt on top of the round device. "You have to make sure the camouflaged antenna isn't covered up so that a signal can be sent back to this black box." He patted the receiver, which looked like it was the base of a PRC-25 radio.

The captain tilted the box so that the team leaders could see the digital display. "Each one of the sensors has been coded to send a signal that will register a number here on the dial. It's important that the sensors are implanted in the right order and that good direction has been recorded; for example, let's use these three sensors. I've lined them up east and west. Let's say the trail is running in that direction. I place this sensor to the west and twenty meters away, this one and, twenty more meters away, the last one." He looked up to see if the men were paying attention, then continued. "Let's say the NVA are moving down the trail from the west headed east. The first sensor will send back its signal number, which is twenty-four. The number twenty-four will appear on the receiver, and then the number forty-four, which is the center sensor. So that's how we know what direction they're moving in. The last sensor will report its number last, of course . . . fifty-four."

"What happens if number fifty-four never comes on?" Fitzpatrick didn't trust devices; he was a recon man from way back and believed that only people could report accurate information.

"One of two things: the device isn't functioning properly; or the NVA took a break and stopped before they reached the last device. *These* devices have been tested and they *work*. If we can get them in the ground around the Special Forces camp, a lot of friendly lives are going to be saved, and the camp will have an early warning system."

"If the Green Berets are so damn good, why don't they bury these things themselves?" Fitzpatrick was trying to be sarcastic, but it was a good question.

"Because they don't want the Strikers or the Vietnamese Special Forces to know about the seismic detectors . . . not right now. They think they have an NVA informer in their camp and they're trying to uncover him."

"Great! Fucking great! A VC spy in the A-camp and

they know we're coming, right?" Fitzpatrick didn't like that idea at all.

"They think we're just *training* with the Special Forces. Each one of our recon teams will have one of the Special Forces men attached from the team as an *instructor,* but actually they'll act as guides to show us where they want these things." The captain looked hard at Fitzpatrick before continuing. "This mission is very important for the Cav! I want all of you to gather as much information as you can about that place. There're rumors that the 1st Brigade is going to be sent there soon, and these devices can end up saving some of *our* asses!"

Arnason spoke seriously. "I've heard that the A Shau is a real tough place to patrol; steep mountains and valleys that are so overgrown with bamboo and vines that you can spend hours hacking your way a couple of meters. Is that true?"

"Yes, and add to that the heavy fog . . . every morning and every night." The captain shook his head and looked back at the map. "The A Shau Valley runs basically north and south, and the winds go west to east mostly. The valley holds in the moisture and fog. The mountainsides are almost constantly wet, and the air is hot during the day and freezing at night. Things *grow* so damn fast there that you had better not fall asleep on the ground!" He tried making a joke, but it never left the floor.

"What is the team breakdown?" Arnason was wondering how many of their recon teams were being used for the mission.

"Two heavy teams of five men each." The captain went over to the chalkboard and wrote out the names

FITZPATRICK	REED
JAMES	ARNASON

FILLMORE   BARNETT
KIRKPATRICK   WOODS
BROWN   SINCLAIR

"Plus you'll be assigned one of the Special Forces sergeants when you fly into the camp." The captain was waiting for Arnason's reaction to the assignment. Lieutenant
Reed was detailed to go along to set up the receiver system
and to command the joint teams. Arnason had never been
second-in-command of a recon team, and the captain was
expecting to receive some flack from him. "Any questions?"

Arnason remained sitting quietly in his seat. Lieutenant
Reed avoided looking over in his direction. He was the one
who recommended that he lead Arnason's team instead of
Fitzpatrick's. The captain had originally assigned him to
the senior NCO's team so that Fitzpatrick could keep an
eye on the junior lieutenant, but Reed had requested the
change; he knew that Arnason had the better team.

"No questions?" The captain was thankful that Arnason
hadn't made a scene. "Have your teams ready to load up
tomorrow morning at 0630 for their flight to Da Nang and
then to A Shau." The captain left the team leaders and
went back to his office. Arnason went over and picked up
the sensor; he hefted it in one hand to judge its weight and
was satisfied that they could easily carry it.

"I think this was a great idea." Reed held up the antenna. "It looks exactly like a new bamboo shoot." He
waited until Fitzpatrick left before continuing. "I hope
you're not mad over my taking over your team for this
mission, Sergeant."

Arnason looked the officer directly in the eyes and held
his stare for a good minute before answering. "My men are
soldiers and will obey orders. Just don't get them killed,

Lieutenant." Arnason left the officer standing in front of the table alone.

Barnett didn't hold his feeling back. He didn't like the idea of a new lieutenant taking over the team, and the only thing that kept him from telling the lieutenant what he thought was that Sergeant Arnason was still going along on the mission as second-in-command of the team and third in the chain for the mission.

The two teams waited on the helipad while the captain and the lieutenant talked in private near the command bunker and tactical operations center. Woods watched and wondered what they were talking about that was taking so long. The sun was beginning to warm up as it climbed over the buildings. The captain poked the young ROTC lieutenant in the chest with his finger, and Woods could see that the older officer was lecturing him. Woods shook his head and tapped Barnett, getting him to observe the pair of officers.

"Fuck this shit!" Barnett grabbed his backpack and started walking over to their assigned CH-47 for the ride to Da Nang where they were going to load up some supplies for the A-camp and go in with it. Barnett's pack was heavy with the additional weight of the seismic detector.

"Let's load up!" Arnason was getting impatient. The captain had been talking to the lieutenant for almost an hour. None of them knew that the brigade commander had called the recon leader into his office late the night before and had briefed him on the message he had received almost two weeks earlier concerning James's activities at the Recondo School in Nha Trang. The captain had been very angry that it had taken so long to get to him, and now James was on a very important mission and the captain was trying to instruct his lieutenant on what he wanted done.

"Do you understand, Lieutenant Reed?" The captain's

voice bordered on panicking. "I don't want either of the
NCOs to know about what we suspect James is doing on
patrol in the field! It's too late to switch you over to Fitzpatrick's team without causing a lot of suspicion, but I
want you to watch James as much as you can, and if we
lose anybody to enemy fire, I want you to investigate the
kind of weapon that killed them." The captain patted
Reed's shoulder like a football coach would do to one of
his players in whom he had little confidence but was being
forced to rely on. "When you get back, I'll confront James
and we'll take it from there."

"Here he comes!" Woods was glad that they could get
under way. The hardest part of running recon was the flight
to the infiltration site. This mission would be easy in that
respect because they were going to fly directly into a Special Forces A-camp and sneak out during the night. That
was a hell of a lot better than going into a hot LZ.

Reed dropped his backpack down next to Barnett's seat
and waved to the crew chief of the large twin-rotor helicopter that they were ready to leave. The machine shook and
started lifting off the pad. Barnett pushed his pack across
the aisle and took a seat away from the lieutenant. He
made no bones about how he felt and wasn't about to give
the officer any slack until the man had proven himself
worthy of Arnason's command.

The Chinooks cruised at about a hundred and forty kilometers an hour and made excellent time to Da Nang. The
Special Forces C-team supply people loaded up ammunition
and hand flares, along with three live cows and a dozen crates
of live chickens and ducks. Woods grinned and didn't com-
plain after he saw the load Fitzpatrick's chopper got: a dozen
large pigs that stunk up the whole chopper because they
needed to fly with the rear tailgate up.

Barnett had joined the side door gunner on the flight out

to the A Shau and leaned out of the window to watch the terrain below them. He could see where Marines and ARVN forces had carved fire-support bases out of the jungle. The hilltops they occupied were brown and red clay that contrasted with the dark green jungle surrounding them. As they neared the Laotian border, Air Force B-52 arc-light missions had left the jungle scarred for stretches that were over two miles long and a half mile wide. The arc-light missions were terrifying to troops on the ground. The two-thousand-pound bombs would shake the ground as far away from the bombing site as five thousand meters.

The lead Chinook made a large circle around the small A-camp, and once it had located the helipad and saw the friendly smoke, it dropped down through the low-hanging clouds and made a good landing. Barnett went over to the other side of the chopper and checked to see if the ground fog was as thick over there as it was on the other side and saw that the whole valley seemed coated in the heavy gray cloud. It was almost noon, and the fog was still there. Barnett didn't like it; the drifting fog gave an ominous signal to the alert recon man.

A group of men left the protection of the lean-to that acted as a supply tent and kitchen for the two hundred commandos living in the enclosure. Barnett noticed that the Americans were wearing wet-weather gear and the commandos who were helping unload the animals were wearing indigenous ponchos that were designed for their smaller stature. It wasn't raining, but everything was damp and mildewed.

Arnason unloaded his team and took them over to a CONEX bunker the Special Forces NCO had pointed out to him before he joined the other SF men unloading the choppers. Arnason noticed that even the team officers helped in the task.

* * *

She lay on the large wet rock that jutted out from the side of the mountain and licked her paws. The loud noise of the Chinooks had made her nervous, but she enjoyed the slight warmth coming from the rock and growled a warning to the machines to keep their distance. She watched the helicopters land in the valley below, and a faint odor of good-smelling meat reached her on the strong breeze after a few minutes. The cows smelled almost like the deer she used to eat, and the pigs were a very familiar smell. She licked her nose and then yawned. She wasn't hungry; the night before she had found plenty of food after the bright little flashes had appeared in the jungle outside of the human enclosure.

Barnett looked up at the mountainside and shuddered. He knew that a great danger was waiting out there, and he couldn't identify it, which made it even worse.

Woods saw the look on his teammate's face and looked at the spot at which Barnett was staring; neither of them could see the large female tiger on the ledge. "Something wrong, Spence?" Woods squinted his eyes and still couldn't see the perfectly camouflaged animal.

Barnett kept looking at the spot on the mountainside. "Naw, just a little nervous, is all." He reached down and picked up his pack.

Arnason smelled the heavy air. He didn't like the place, either. He had heard a lot of stories about the A Shau Valley and now he believed them. The valley had been the Vietcong's and the property of the Viet Minh, who had fought against the French. The extremely bad weather made it almost impossible to hold the valley against a ground force. Artillery worked poorly, and support aircraft could only fly in less than four days out of the month, and that was during the *dry* season!

The Green Beret captain led the ten men from the cav into the command bunker that doubled as the American sleeping quarters. Three CONEX containers had been placed side by side, and three more of the large steel shipping crates were lined up about ten feet away from the first three, with their openings facing in toward the center. Huge beams had been laid on the roofs of the containers, and the PSP laced on top of them was covered with eight layers of sandbags. The ends of the long tunnel were sealed off except for the doors at each end. It was an easy bunker to make and took only a few hard hours to assemble.

Arnason looked around the command bunker as the captain briefed the teams. The Green Beret communications sergeant slept in the same CONEX container as his radios, and the medic had set up his medical operation out of his CONEX also. Arnason guessed that the Vietnamese Special Forces medics had done the same and that there was a dispensary setup for the commandos. The Green Beret captain's voice caught Arnason's attention. He noticed that the officer spoke as if he were fighting for the strength just to speak. There had been no friendly greetings when they entered the A-camp, and no offers of beer. Arnason looked at the drawn faces of the other Special Forces men and realized that the team was under a great deal of strain.

"I'm going to send out my intelligence NCO with one of your teams and my executive officer." The captain saw the look on Barnett's face and added, "They're the only two men left in this camp who can still hump the mountains. Everyone else is either sick with one kind or the other of fucking jungle rot, or has been wounded and will be flying out of here with the Chinooks."

The sound of the large choppers leaving the camp accented the captain's words. A very sad look filled the officer's eyes. He must have been in his late twenties but looked fifty. "That leaves me with three SF men still able to function." The captain's eyes found Woods's. "Needless to say, we really need those seismic devices installed as soon as possible." He inhaled a deep breath and continued. "What I recommend, Lieutenant, is that you get those things in the ground and get back here as soon as you possibly can . . ." He left the sentence unfinished.

Lieutenant Reed spoke. "It sounds like there's a lot of action around here."

The captain's eyes spoke for him. The bunker became very quiet.

"Well, we had better get our stuff together and get ready to leave tonight." Reed looked back at the captain. "Is there going to be a moon tonight?"

The look the captain gave the lieutenant wasn't meant to be insulting, but it was a look of pure pity. "The fog blocks out all the light after two in the morning. You had better be where you want to go by then. My men have been to the sites before, so it shouldn't be too difficult, except for the climb." The captain went to the entrance and paused. He didn't look back but spoke loud enough for everyone to hear him. "I've got to check my guards."

"That's one weird officer!" Fitzpatrick spit a stream of tobacco juice on the PSP floor and caught a dirty glare from the SF medic, who had been watching from his hootch. "Sorry about that!" Fitzpatrick tried using his boot heel to spread out the brown stain.

Barnett sipped from his canteen and handed it to Woods. The very last rays of sunlight were a shining sliver on the inside edge of the eastern mountain. The two recon men watched as the light slipped away; it would only be a few more minutes, and it would be dark enough to leave the camp undetected by any close-in enemy observers. The plan for the first night's move was to get just far enough away from the camp so as not to be seen leaving it and have their direction of travel monitored by the NVA.

Barnett didn't look at Woods when he spoke. He didn't trust his eyes. "David, I don't feel good about this one. . . ."

"Now don't start that shit with me! Man! I'm fucking ready to shit my pants, and you start with the weird talk!" Woods slapped Barnett's shoulder. "Fucking fight 'em, man . . . that's what *Cav* recon does! Fuck and fight!"

"David, promise me that you won't leave me alone out there alive." Barnett didn't have to go into detail; Woods knew exactly what his teammate was saying.

"Only if you promise me the same thing," Woods almost whispered. The bravado of his earlier statement was gone.

"It's a deal." Barnett left Woods and moved quickly toward the gate. He wanted to be alone for a few minutes.

The two Special Forces team members from the A Shau camp acted as the point men for the recon teams and led the way through the thick grass. The very first thing Woods noticed when they had cleared the A-camp was the smell of the valley. It was a smell that none of the team members would ever forget as long as they lived. Wet, rotting wood and damp moss was the best way to describe the odor of the thick jungle. It was not an unpleasant smell, just distinctive and unforgettable.

Woods constantly lost sight of the reflective tape on the back of Barnett's soft jungle cap, and a couple of times he felt a deep anxiety and panic spring up when he lost sight of the reflective tape for more than few seconds. Sinclair bumped into him once in the darkness, which reassured Woods that he wasn't the only one having problems seeing in the dark; Sinclair was the *best* rear guard in the world.

A muffled fall told Arnason's team that Fitzpatrick was still traveling about a hundred meters away to their left flank. The teams were moving up the mountain on two separate fingers of rock and underbrush. The SF men had selected their night trails well and needed only to feel the pull of the mountain against their legs to know in which direction they were traveling on the steep slope.

Lieutenant Reed had wanted to split the teams up, with each element taking a different side of the valley to place the sensors, but a combined effort on the part of the Special Forces men convinced him that it was dangerous enough sending twelve men out together where companies feared to tread. What made the A Shau such a difficult terrain to maneuver in was the thick jungle and the dense fog. Once a unit made contact with the NVA, they were on their own for resupplies, artillery support, and most importantly, air support. The wounded usually died in the A Shau Valley, but that went for the NVA too.

Woods bumped into Barnett's backpack and felt like a fool until Sinclair bumped into him. Barnett reached back, grabbed Woods, and pulled him toward the tight group. Woods reached back until he located Sinclair and pulled him into the small circle of heads. The Special Forces sergeant whispered very low but still could be heard. "We stay here tonight. Form a star."

Woods could feel that the ground had leveled off, and guessed that they were on the military crest of the mountain or a decent-sized ledge. He remembered the star team position from Recondo School and felt in the dark for the man on each side of him, then lay down with his legs spread apart until they touched the legs of the men next to him. The lager position was excellent for nights like this one where you couldn't see your own hand touching your nose; it also made you feel more secure when you could touch another person.

The fog rolled in without being seen but could be felt like a wet blanket touching bare skin. Barnett had sat Indian-style during his two hours on watch and now leaned over to wake Woods for the last shift right before dawn. He paused and sniffed the air, then shook Woods gently awake. Barnett sniffed the air again and was sure this time; someone was smoking grass. He leaned over and whispered in Woods's ear. Woods sniffed the air and agreed; someone was smoking dope. He whispered to Barnett. "VC?"

Barnett cupped his hands over Woods's ear and whispered back, "Fuck, no . . . someone on Fitz's team!"

The morning light surprised everyone except the Green Beret; he'd experienced it before. The ground fog was so thick that they couldn't see three feet away. It was as if they were floating in a cloud. Woods looked down and couldn't see his boots. He could see a vague outline of Arnason a few feet away, then knelt down until he could see Barnett sleeping on the ground, rolled up in his poncho. Sinclair came into view, and he woke both of them and used hand signals to inform them that they were moving out in ten minutes. Barnett rolled over on his side and unbuttoned his pants to urinate. He released his bladder lying on his side, then got up on his feet.

Woods eased over to Arnason and whispered softly in his ear. "Did you smell someone smoking dope last night?"

Arnason shook his head in the negative.

"We did . . . between 0400 and dawn." Woods nodded in the direction of Fitzpatrick's team.

Arnason flexed his jaws and glared at Woods, then he pulled his team member over so that he could whisper back. "I'll handle it when we meet up with them the day after tomorrow."

David nodded and reached down for his backpack. His muscles were sore from the difficult climb and sleeping all night on the damp ground.

The mist was scary to be walking in, but not as bad as it

had been while traveling the night before. The sun burned the fog off the mountaintops early in the day, and a beautiful array of mountain vegetation replaced the prior night's fear with wonder. Brilliant flowers and dark green plants reflected the sunlight. Woods forgot his fears of the night and actually enjoyed the patrol until they reached their first site. The task of digging holes in the rocky soil was almost impossible, and twice they had to move down the trail until they could find a suitable location. Woods noticed the weight difference in his pack as soon as he had buried his first sensor and screwed in the device's antenna.

The open trail was making the whole team nervous, and even though Woods couldn't see Sergeant Arnason or the Green Beret sergeant, he knew that they were down the trail acting as guards for them. Woods took a few seconds to observe the wide path that ran along the top of the jagged mountain range. The NVA had used the trail frequently, and even artillery fires would have a difficult time scoring a direct hit because a long or a short round would miss the trail by hundreds of meters because of the razorback ridge. The NVA knew what they were doing when they had picked the A Shau Valley as a stronghold.

Arnason and Sinclair came down the trail moving in crouches low to the trail; they signaled for the team to take cover, and instantly the recon patrol melted into the surrounding jungle. A group of five NVA walking next to modified bicycles appeared on the trail and disappeared just as suddenly. Woods had gotten a quick glimpse of the technique they were using and was impressed. The NVA had tied metal rods across the handlebars of the bikes, and the rider, rather than sitting on the seat, walked next to the bike and steered it with one hand on the rod and the other hand holding on to the bundle of supplies that was balanced where the seat used to be. The bikes could haul heavy loads over rough terrain quickly and safely.

Arnason stepped out on the trail and listened. He waited, then signaled for the team to join him. Slowly the men emerged from the jungle and started moving down the trail in the opposite direction in which the NVA had gone. It would be almost totally impossible to travel on the side of the mountain, parallel to the trail. You either used the trail with extreme caution or you went all the way back down the side of the mountain to the valley floor and then moved down there parallel to the mountaintop, before climbing all the way back up again.

Five more times during the day the team slipped off the trail into the jungle. The more they did the disappearing act, the better they got at it and the more confident they became. The Green Beret sergeant signaled that they had reached their last site for the sensors, and this time it was much easier digging the devices in and camouflaging them. Lieutenant Reed checked each one of the sensors before they left them to insure that they were in working condition.

The Green Beret captain watched the digital readout panel on the seismic-intrusion detector-receiver. He punched in the code for a test, and three sets of numbers flashed on the screen. All but one set of sensors was operating. The captain checked his map and marked in grease pencil the third location in blue, which indicated that the system was up and operating. He stared at the map and wondered if any of the Cav recon men had guessed yet that they were operating in Laos.

Barnett and Woods used the large, exposed root of a hardwood tree for a backrest and untied one of the side straps on their packs to remove the small plastic bags of indigenous rations the Special Forces team had supplied. The Vietnamese food was much better than the LRRP rations and provided a higher level of protein, especially the meal of dehydrated fish and rice. What the Cav recon teams had noticed almost immediately were the *soft* plastic packages the meals were packed in, which didn't make any noise when you opened them. The American LRRP rations had been designed by a team of people who had never served in the field and most certainly not with a recon patrol. The LRRP rations were wrapped in a tinfoil-type pouch that made a lot of noise when you tried opening them. Recon teams improvised by cutting the tops off the rations before they went out on patrol, and then they added water just before they ate the food. The Special Forces teams went one step further; large combat units could get away with carrying dry rations and stopping near streams and rivers to get water, but small recon teams had to premix the dehydrated meals before they left on patrol because they couldn't risk hunting for streams and rivers; not all of the meals were mixed with water on long patrols, but at least two packages were rehydrating at all times.

Woods squeezed the rice-and-fish mix out of the plastic tube directly into his mouth without using a spoon. He hadn't realized just how hungry he was until the food reached his stomach. He ate all of the first meal and was considering the second one when Arnason signaled to get ready to move out. It was Woods's turn to carry the PRC-77 secure-voice radio, and he hurried to transfer it from Sinclair's pack to his before the team started heading toward the preselected rendezvous site with Fitzpatrick's team.

The Special Forces sergeant struggled to his feet using his weapon as a cane. The man was almost totally exhausted and was functioning on sheer guts and large doses of amphetamines. He had spent seven months at the A Shau camp without ever having left it, except to go on combat patrols that averaged an eighty percent chance of making contact with the enemy and to pull twenty-hour

workdays building the A-camp when he wasn't on patrol.
Barnett went over to the sergeant and used hand signals to
say that he was taking over the point. The sergeant became
angry and shook his head that it was too dangerous. Barnett persisted, and the sergeant finally gave in and let the
young soldier take over the strenuous and nerve-racking
task of breaking point.

Lieutenant Reed hadn't interfered during the whole patrol and had allowed for the sergeants to make the deci-
sions, especially the Special Forces NCO, who knew the
area that they were patrolling in. Reed had saved face by
not making a scene over who commanded the team. Barnett's demanding that he be allowed to take point had made
the officer feel guilty, and he tried to intervene and take the
point from him. It was a mistake. The young soldier abso-
lutely refused to give the critical position of point man up
to the lieutenant.

The team stopped when the sun was halfway up the side
of the mountain on the opposite side of the valley. Arnason
checked his map with the SF sergeant, and they both
agreed that they were very close to the meeting site. Arnason signaled that the team should stay where they were,
and then he beckoned for Woods to join him for a short
reconnoiter of the immediate area. He knew that he was
within a couple hundred meters of the site.

The normal jungle noises comforted Woods as the two
of them moved slowly through the thick undergrowth.
The jungle was triple-canopied, with huge hardwood
trees poking up through the thick growth of secondary
trees. Woods felt secure and moved behind the sergeant
with excellent stealth. The two of them had gone less
than a hundred meters when Arnason came to an abrupt
halt and took a half step backward toward Woods, who
instinctively flipped the safety off his CAR-15 and
searched for the enemy.

Arnason signaled with his hand for Woods to join him
without looking back. The sight that met Woods's eyes was
almost unbelievable. The jungle had been leveled in an
almost perfect fifty-foot circle. Every blade of grass, every
bush or vine, had been torn up. The ground was bare of
even the common dark green moss. Arnason risked whispering, "What do you think did this?"

Woods shrugged his shoulders and shook his head
slowly from side to side. He had no idea. A bomb would
have left a crater, and artillery would have shattered the
bushes and trees, leaving scars high up on the hardwood.
Everything had been leveled that was underbrush, and the
large trees were untouched. The wind changed direction
slightly, and both of the recon men caught a whiff of something rotting. Arnason led the way around the perimeter of
the circle and stopped when he reached the decomposing
male tiger.

"Looks like something ate half of it." Woods wrinkled
his nose and tried not breathing in the obnoxious smell.

Arnason slipped down into a battle crouch and surveyed
the immediate area. "It looks like two tigers had one hell of
a battle here." He nodded back to the way they had come.
"Let's get out of here."

Woods took the lead, and they circled around the open
area. The rendezvous site was located about a hundred
meters from the tiger battleground. The two recon men
rested for a few minutes and took their time checking out
the jungle around the meeting place before returning to
bring back the rest of their team.

Lieutenant Reed selected the night positions for the
team. He put Woods and Barnett together, and Arnason
with Sinclair; the Special Forces sergeant stayed with him
in the position nearest the ridge line and the NVA trail.
Reed was trying to make up for not humping the point and
figured he would take the night watch by himself and let

the sergeant rest. He had preselected three additional sites for Fitzpatrick's team when they arrived. The compiled teams would remain on the narrow finger of ground for the night and until the heavy fog burned off in the morning before returning to the A-camp. A day entry wouldn't matter; their mission would be completed by then.

Arnason's team took turns sleeping during the afternoon. Woods couldn't believe how deep he slept, lying in the warm sunlight. When he awoke, he felt like shit, but after a few minutes he could feel the positive effects the deep REM sleep had had on him. He was alert and rested.

Arnason waved for Woods to join him. Sinclair was sleeping soundly, along with the SF sergeant, who looked as if he had died with his mouth hanging open. Reed felt bad about having to wake the sergeant twice; he had started snoring loudly each time he had slipped into a deep sleep. Woods knelt down next to Arnason and bent over so the sergeant didn't have to get up.

"Fitz should have been here by now. If he doesn't show up in an hour, we've got to go look for him." Arnason didn't like the idea, but Fitzpatrick and the Special Forces lieutenant could have gotten lost.

Woods nodded and returned to his position. He didn't like the idea of going back down the trail, especially with night beginning to fall and whatever had killed that tiger still out there. The more he thought about the lager site, the better he liked the selection. The narrow finger of rock, bamboo, and moss patches would be easy to protect from three sides, and the portion that connected with the mountainside was narrow enough to defend against everything but a large determined enemy force. He looked down the rock side of the ridge and decided that if he had to, he could slide down it for a couple hundred meters, escape, and evade, but only if he really had to.

Sinclair saw the point man first and tapped Arnason

awake. Fitzpatrick's team had arrived just as it was getting dark and stumbled into the small lager area.

"Oh, fuck! What a hump!" Fitzpatrick almost broke out in a normal voice.

"Here . . ." Arnason handed him his canteen full of cold water.

Fitzpatrick drained the container and looked at his friend. "Where did you find *cold* water?"

Arnason leaned over and whispered. "About five meters over there," he said, pointing, "is a small stream that comes out of the mountain. You'll hear it before you see it."

Fitzpatrick signaled for his team to follow him, and they all refilled their canteens and watered down good before returning to where Arnason waited. James and Brown brought up the rear, water still dripping off their chins from where they had washed their faces. Arnason could see the cool water had made a big difference in their morale. He showed them their selected night lager sites that had been partially prepared for them. When it had started getting late, Arnason and Sinclair had stacked some of the smaller boulders into semicircles in each of the positions and figured Fitz's team could finish the job when they got there.

Fitzpatrick put Brown and Kirkpatrick at one fighting point, and Fillmore and James at the other. He stayed with the SF officer, even though he didn't want to spend the night with him, but the night before, when he'd stayed with James, he had caught him smoking dope. Fitz liked his stuff but not in the field.

Fitz's team had barely removed their backpacks when the darkness slipped in. There was no gradual darkening in the jungle. One minute it was dim light under the canopy, and within ten minutes it was pitch-black, especially in the high mountains when the sun slipped behind a ridge line.

Woods took the first watch, and for a couple of hours he

heard soft rustling coming from Fitz's team as they ate and tried improving their positions, but around midnight the perimeter became quiet. Once during the night an NVA unit on the trail passed, making a lot of loud noise. David let Barnett sleep an extra three hours before waking him. It was two in the morning, and instead of breaking up the night in two shifts each, he thought the extra-long rest would be good for Barnett, who never complained, but Woods knew he was exhausted from taking the point all day. He reached over to wake him, then decided on letting him sleep until he got tired. Woods sat Indian-style, his poncho liner wrapped around his shoulders. He thought of home and going back to college. Life was going to be sweet after the war, and he had decided that he wasn't going to waste a single minute of it.

Woods opened his eyes. He was instantly angry for falling asleep. He listened to the night sounds. Something had woken him up. He felt for his CAR-15 on his lap and found it. He listened harder to the night sounds and heard nothing unusual. The hair on the back of his neck rose and sent a shiver down his spine. Something was wrong. He tried thinking if he had dreamed and couldn't remember. He sat alert for over a half hour, then relaxed his back against the rocks. It must have been a bad dream. A sour taste filled his mouth, and he felt next to his leg for his plastic canteen and unscrewed the top. His hearing was so fine-tuned that he heard the small grains of dirt grinding under the cap. Woods placed the opening to his mouth and took a sip.

The scream caused his arm to jerk, and he poured water down the front of his jacket.

Barnett jerked up from his damp bed. "Wha-what!"

"Help me! Oh, God, please help me! Ahhhhhh . . ."

Barnett searched in the dark for Woods. "What's going

on?" He was disoriented in the dark and had burst out from a deep sleep.

Woods had his CAR-15 pointed in the direction of the screaming man. "Shit! I don't know. It sounds like Fillmore."

"*Help . . . oh! Help me . . . Sarge!*" The voice sounded as if it were moving away from them and *down* the side of the mountain.

A short burst from an M-16, followed by a long one, filled the jungle.

It became quiet.

The darkness closed in even darker, and Woods could feel Barnett pressing against his side. He was glad; if Barnett hadn't found him, he would have found Barnett. They were scared—more than scared, they were scared shitless.

Arnason realized that his team was on the verge of panicking, and in a calm voice he called out that everything was all right and he would check it out. The effect was instantaneous. Woods and Barnett took up firing positions and waited. Sinclair pushed off the safety on his weapon and squinted his eyes, trying to see in the dark. The team was ready to fight.

Arnason crawled over to Fillmore and James's position and felt a hot M16 shell under his hand. He couldn't see, but he knew that he was near and whispered softly.

"James?"

There was no answer.

"James?" Arnason heard the heavy breathing and reached out and touched James's boot. "James, you all right?"

There was a long pause, and then James answered, "Oh, fuck, man. Oh, fuck . . ."

Arnason crawled up next to the man and reached along

his body until he felt his collar. He shook him gently. "What happened?"

"I . . . I was sleeping. Fillmore kicked me—he kicked me *hard*—and then the next thing I heard was him screaming!"

"Shh, it's okay!" Arnason could feel the man shaking in his hands.

"It wasn't no NVA—" James's voice broke. "That motherfucking thing *growled*!"

Arnason let go of James's jacket. He knew what had happened: Fillmore had been taken from his position by a tiger. The thought made him feel sick. What a horrible fucking way to die.

No one slept the rest of the night. The two Special Forces men didn't need to be told what had happened. There had been incidents before on patrol at night where a tiger had circled their perimeter for hours before leaving, but it had never attacked before. The Bru tribesmen had reported sighting a large female tiger in the area, but no one took them seriously because she would have to weigh close to seven hundred pounds from their description of her, and the very largest Asian tiger ever recorded weighed only five hundred.

Morning came with sighs of relief from the recon teams. The light took the fear away. Reed called all of the men together, and he explained what had happened to Fillmore. There was no time to search for his body because the NVA had surely heard James's M16 firing and would be coming after them in force. It was now a matter of survival for all of them. Reed seemed calmer than he should have been, but then again he was probably maturing as a combat leader. Arnason grinned. There was hope for the young officer, after all.

The combined teams loaded up their gear and formed into a single line to move down the mountainside. The Special Forces lieutenant insisted on taking the point, and Sinclair automatically found his position in the rear. Woods watched Lieutenant Reed's back and waited for the officer to start moving so that he could follow. They were going to take the shortest way possible down to the A Shau Valley floor, and then make a dash for the A-camp. The lieutenant told them that the point was too steep to travel down safely, even though that was the way the tigress had gone with Fillmore. The plan was to leave the night lager site on the point and then hit the trail for a couple hundred meters until they could find a site on the side of the mountain that wasn't so steep.

The Chicom thirty-six-inch claymore killed the two Special Forces men and Fitzpatrick instantly. James was knocked unconscious from the blast, and Kirkpatrick took a single ball bearing through the palm of his left hand.

Barnett was the first one to react to the NVA ambush that had been waiting for the recon team to come off the finger of rock. The ambush was nearly perfect, except the NVA officer had acted too soon; if he would have waited another couple of minutes, the second team would have been cut off from an escape back to the ridge. Two NVA fell backward from their hiding places behind a hardwood tree as Spencer raked the surrounding jungle with a long burst from his CAR-15.

Arnason threw two hand grenades and killed the team that had detonated the claymore.

Kirkpatrick was struggling with Brown's body when Lieutenant Reed backed up into them. "Let's go! He's dead!"

Kirkpatrick's eyes widened. *"No!* I can't leave him here!"

"Let's go! We'll come back and get him later!" Reed pushed Kirkpatrick back toward the last safe place he knew, the ridge line. A single NVA twisted around the edge of a tree, and Reed caught him across the chest with a short burst.

Arnason, Barnett, and Woods walked backward and laid down a heavy, suppressive fire while they retreated back to their old fighting positions.

The NVA officer barked orders to his platoon, and the air whistled with AK-47 rounds cutting through the brush, and Chicom hand grenades exploding.

Woods dropped down on one knee to change magazines, and Barnett covered for him. Lieutenant Reed and Kirkpatrick broke out of the jungle right in front of them, and Barnett almost shot them but waved them past instead.

Sinclair had still been waiting on the ridge for the column to clear the area when the claymore had detonated and he still hadn't fired a round. He watched as Reed and Kirkpatrick stumbled back toward him. He could see Woods's and Barnett's backs, and then Arnason appeared through the dark green brush.

"Over here!" Sinclair threw one of his hand grenades and called out again, "*Over here!*"

The remainder of the recon teams stumbled back toward the familiar voice. Sinclair hadn't been wasting his time. He had set up the two claymore mines he was carrying and had drawn his team members back between them.

There was a pause in the firing. The NVA commander was regrouping his force. Arnason dropped down next to Sinclair. "We're going down the side of the ravine."

Sinclair nodded. "Let me blast these first."

"No! You go. I'll be the rear guard!" Barnett shoved Sinclair hard in the direction in which the rest of the team had gone.

"I'm the rear guard!" Sinclair growled the words out.

"Not today. Someone has to take care of the *kids*!"

That was the *only* thing Barnett could have said that would have made Sinclair leave the claymores.

Sinclair's eyes changed focus for a second, and then he took off after Arnason. The NVA opened fire from the jungle, and a round caught Sinclair in the back just below his shoulder blade. He flipped forward from the impact and rolled back up onto his feet. There was no pain, only a numbness in his side.

Barnett squatted down and laid his CAR-15 across his legs. He held a claymore detonator in each hand and waited. A slight sound to his left rear drew his attention, and he glanced over in that direction. Woods crouched with his CAR-15 at the ready.

"Get the fuck out of here. I'll follow as soon as I blast these!" Barnett looked back in the direction of the NVA.

Woods saw the NVA coming first, and fired a long burst. The blast from the claymores deafened both of the Americans. Barnett got up on his feet and started down the ridge line with Woods fighting a brief rear action. His CAR-15 popped, signaling that it was empty. He started running down the team's path and saw Barnett waiting. As soon as he passed him, he heard Barnett's CAR-15. Woods ran hard until he reached Arnason, who was trying to drag Sinclair to the edge of the ravine. Woods grabbed hold of Sinclair's web harness on one side, and Arnason grabbed the other and they went over the edge. The loose gravel gave way, and the three of them slid a hundred meters before any of them could gain a foothold.

Spencer saw the pack of NVA break free of the jungle a dozen feet in front of him. He couldn't hear anything because of the claymore blasts. He squeezed his CAR-15's trigger and a three-round burst came out, then the weapon was empty. He reached for his Browning 9-mm when the first NVA hit him and was instantly joined by three more. Spencer struggled and fought hard, but there were too many of them. The last thing he remembered was the blurred image of something coming toward his head, and then everything went blank.

Woods let go of Sinclair as soon as they had stopped sliding on the loose rock and immediately started trying to climb back up the steep incline. Arnason grabbed him and threw him down on the sharp rocks, but Woods didn't feel any pain.

"I've got to go back and help Spencer!"

"We'll wait for him down in the valley!"

"*No!*"

"*Go!*" Arnason shoved Woods in the direction of the valley floor and the remaining team members.

"I can't leave Spencer. I promised him!"

"If he's still alive, he'll make it . . . just like we did!"

Woods thought for a second and realized that there was no way he could climb back up the loose rocks.

Arnason broke Woods's indecision. "Help me with Sinclair or he won't make it!"

Woods slung his CAR-15 over his shoulder, grabbed Sinclair by his harness, and helped Arnason drag him to cover seconds before a dozen Chicom grenades and three American M-26s came flying over the edge of the ridge down to where they had been standing in the loose gravel. The explosions echoed along the valley floor and could be heard in the A-camp.

The Special Forces captain stood in the doorway of his command bunker and looked up at the mountainside. He was wondering how many of the men from the recon teams would return. All of the seismic-intrusion devices were working perfectly, and they had already been sending back information; what none of the recon team members knew was that one of each set of sensors was a top-secret audio transmitter that was designed especially to monitor sound along the highly used Ho Chi Minh Trail.

S E V E N

Prisoner of War

The Special Forces captain led the relief force himself.
He used the knoll to the west of his A-camp as a reference
point and didn't need to use his lensatic compass once. He
led a company of Tau-Oi, a tough group of fighting men.
The C-team was sending him two MIKE Force companies
of Nungs out of Da Nang to reinforce his rescue attempt,
and the 1st Cavalry Division had promised an infantry battalion as soon as one was available.

The captain pushed his lead element hard. The weather
was good, but in the A Shau, that could change with a
wind shift. He wanted to have the landing zone secured as
soon as possible for the MIKE Force. He knew from prior
experience that they would only make *one* attempt to land,
then would be forced to return to Da Nang because they
would be low on fuel.

Arnason kept looking back over his shoulder. He was
praying that there would be more survivors from the ambush. Woods was carrying Sinclair piggyback. The shock
had worn off, and Sinclair was starting to bleed a lot.

Kirkpatrick and Lieutenant Reed broke trail down to the valley floor.

Woods felt the sweat form a stream between his chest muscles and flow down to his belt line where it was absorbed in the cloth. He knew that he couldn't travel far with Sinclair's dead weight bouncing around on his back; besides, he wasn't going to get too far away from Barnett.

Lieutenant Reed stopped and dropped down on one knee. He waited until the rest of the men caught up before speaking. "Let's break here and wait a couple of hours . . . just in case."

Arnason looked around the place the lieutenant had selected. It was a good choice. The rise in the ground they were on gave them a commanding view of the area, and numerous anthills provided protection from grazing fire during an attack. Arnason set up a perimeter with the remaining men. Sinclair was placed in the center of the small circle. Everyone had lost their backpacks during the ambush except Reed, and the only large battle dressing he had was on Sinclair already and saturated with blood. Arnason tried thinking what he could use to stop Sinclair's bleeding and decided on using his fatigue jacket as a sort of chest tourniquet. He emptied his pockets looking for a soft piece of plastic to seal the hole in Sinclair's chest with, and the only thing he could find was the cover he used to keep his children's picture dry. Arnason hesitated for only a second, then pulled the photograph from the plastic and placed the material over the bubbling hole. Lieutenant Reed watched the sergeant work. He squeezed as much blood out of the bandage as he could, placed it back over the wound, tied it snugly, and then tied his jacket around the bandage. It worked; the bleeding slowed down. Arnason opened his left rear ammo pouch that he used for a first-aid kit and removed the last morphine Syrette from its package. He injected the painkiller in Sinclair's left leg and squeezed the small, collapsible tube until it was empty.

Woods left his place on the perimeter where he had dropped down exhausted the instant Sinclair had been helped off his back. He staggered over to where Arnason sat as soon as he caught his breath and growled the words. "I'm going back after Spencer!" It wasn't a request, it was a statement.

"Fine, but let's rest here for a few minutes and I'll go with you." Arnason tried pouring the last of his water from his canteen in Sinclair's mouth, but the soldier turned his head to one side and the water only wet his lips.

Lieutenant Reed heard the conversation, thought for a second, and then spoke. "They must have heard the fire-fight in the A-camp and will be sending a relief force."

"I wouldn't bet on that." Arnason remembered what the captain had said about not having any more men left that weren't sick or wounded.

"I'm going to try to make it back to the A-camp alone." The lieutenant's voice reflected his fear but also the courage it took to make the offer. "Kirkpatrick and Sinclair are wounded, and we can't carry them all the way back. If you and Woods stayed here with them, I could travel fast and be back here no later than tomorrow morning."

Arnason thought for a few minutes. The lieutenant was making good sense. They couldn't outrun the NVA if they were still following them, and Sinclair couldn't take much more of the rough treatment of being carried. He needed to be MEDEVACed. "Go!"

Reed picked up his weapon and left the group without looking back. He was scared, but he wasn't going to let his men down. The first thing that entered his mind when he disappeared into the tall elephant grass was the tigress.

Woods lay on the damp ground so that he could see the mountainside they had just left. He could barely make out the end of the finger of ground on which they had been ambushed. He strained his eyes looking for Barnett.

Arnason crawled over to where Kirkpatrick was stretched out and touched his shoulder. The soldier opened his eyes and almost started crying. "Sarge, are we going to get out of this shit?"

"Bet your 'Rican ass we are!" Arnason smiled. "The worst is over."

"Man, that fucking Chicom claymore cut those guys in half!" Kirkpatrick started crying. "Brown . . . he didn't have a fucking chance. We had just traded places, did you know that?"

"Don't blame yourself." Arnason knew what Kirkpatrick was thinking; he had been there himself. "You can't blame yourself for stuff like that or you'll go crazy."

"Brown and me were going to open a record shop back in Brooklyn when we left this shithole place."

"So you still can open your record shop and you can name it Brown and Kirkpatrick Incorporated."

"I'll do that, Sarge. Thanks." Kirkpatrick rolled over on his stomach and blinked back the tears. He would never let himself make another friend during the war; it hurt too much.

Barnett felt the pain before he opened his eyes. He thought that he had been wounded, but the pain was coming from the way the NVA had tied his hands behind his back on the bamboo pole. He blinked to clear his vision and saw a group of NVA sorting through Sergeant Fitzpatrick's pack and dividing up the food and gear between them. He slowly turned his head to one side and saw his dead teammates lined up in the clearing. They were all in the same position: their arms stretched out over their heads, their pants pulled down past their knees, and their jackets shoved up under their armpits. The NVA had removed their boots and socks. Barnett could see the face of one of the Special Forces men; it was the lieutenant. The officer's eyes were open and his mouth was slightly parted; an iridescent green beetle was walking along his lower lip. The thought passing through his mind was a simple one: So this is how it feels to lose a fight.

The NVA officer looked over and saw that Barnett was awake. He stood up and adjusted the top of his pants before striding up to the American. The NVA lieutenant kicked Barnett to get his attention and saw the glare flash in the young soldier's eyes. He was impressed, thinking that the boy would be terrified when he woke up. He sneered and reached down with both hands and yanked on the bamboo pole, forcing Spencer to his feet. The pain was instant, and Barnett screamed.

The NVA lieutenant grunted and placed his hands on his hips. "You not so *tough,* 'merican boy!" The accent was Vietnamese, laced with French.

Barnett blinked his eyes to clear them of the tears of pain and saw one of the NVA soldiers glaring at him with a look of pure hate. The soldier spoke to the lieutenant in rapid Vietnamese and pointed at him with a shaking finger.

"My soldier say he saw you kill his friend. He want to kill you!" The lieutenant frowned and struggled with the rest of the words. "What you think about that!"

"Fuck you!"

The lieutenant became instantly angry and cuffed Spencer hard against the side of his head. "You say fuck to me! *Respect!* You respect North Vietnamese officer!"

"*Fuck you, comrade!*" Spencer screamed the words at the Communist officer.

The NVA soldiers couldn't understand what Barnett was

yelling, but the tone of his voice was enough for them to figure out that it wasn't respectful.

The officer curled his lip back off his teeth and stuttered out his next sentence. "You say 'fuck'! Okay, 'merican soldier! *You fuck*!" He went over to Sergeant Fitzpatrick's naked body and cut off the NCO's penis. Barnett watched from his position on the ground where two of the NVA soldiers had him pinned down so that he couldn't move.

The lieutenant ordered his men to bring Barnett to his knees and raise his chin. The NVA soldier who had glared at Barnett earlier used a two-foot-long piece of bamboo under Spencer's chin to lift his head up. Spencer was forced to look up at the officer by the pressure against his back from the NVA soldier's knee and the pull from the bamboo under his chin. Two more NVA soldiers held him upright under his arms.

"*You like fuck*!" The lieutenant screamed the words. "*Fuck this*!" He pushed the bloody, amputated penis against the young American soldier's lips. "*Fuck*!" He kicked Spencer in the stomach and screamed again. "*Fuck this*!"

Spencer kept his mouth closed and tried breathing through his nose.

The NVA lieutenant wiped the bloody organ over Spencer's face, then threw it back toward the row of American bodies. "*I teach you . . . fuck*!" He kicked and punched Barnett until the soldier passed out from the pain, and when the seventeen-year-old fell over on his side, the NVA soldier who had held his chin kicked him three times in the groin.

The lieutenant went over to the other American prisoner and glared at him before speaking. "You like fuck?"

James looked directly into the NVA's eyes. "No, man.

You're the boss . . . *sir!*"

The lieutenant nodded his head. "You smart!"

Lieutenant Reed met up with the Special Forces captain less than an hour after he had left the remaining members of the team and told him where they were waiting and that they needed a MEDEVAC chopper. The captain called back the information and decided to use the team's location for the landing zone. He remembered the small rise in the valley well from prior patrols, and it was an excellent place to defend. The knoll was far enough away from the mountain so that the NVA small mortars couldn't reach them, and it provided excellent fields of fire for his machine guns.

Arnason saw the relief force first and warned the rest of the team that the commandos were approaching their site. Woods couldn't wait to return back to the ambush site and find Barnett's body. He was hoping that Spencer had escaped and was trying to E&E out of the area, but he would be happy to bring his body back if he had been killed.

The Special Forces captain refused to send out a platoon with Woods and Arnason, and ordered them to stay with him until the MIKE Force arrived and he could send a Nung Company with them.

Corporal Barnett fell down and was yanked back up on his feet by the guards on each side of him. The bamboo pole was tied behind his back and extended out a foot on each side of his elbows. The nylon cord that was tied around each of Spencer's wrists and ran across his belly cut into his skin each time the pole was yanked.

James walked behind Barnett and tried keeping out of the NVA guards' way. He was glad that Barnett was giving the NVA a hard time because they were concentrating all of their hate on him. James sneered every time one of the guards hit the blond-haired honkie or when Barnett screamed from the pain. James would have been really enjoying himself if he wasn't a prisoner also.

Night was beginning to fall, and the NVA lieutenant increased his pace on the trail. Barnett could barely walk from the blows he had taken, especially the kicks he had received in his groin. The lieutenant ordered two of his men to carry Barnett, and they slung their weapons over their backs and lifted the prisoner's pole up on their shoulders. Barnett bounced from the pole with all of his weight centered on the crooks of his elbows. The pain was extraordinary, and with each step the NVA took the teenager screamed until he passed out.

The NVA soldier whose friends Barnett had killed, smiled each time Barnett screamed. He looked over and saw that James was smiling also.

The lieutenant directed his men off the trail and guided them to a series of deep caves in the side of the mountain that gave them protection from even arc-light bombing. James was very interested in the underground structure and almost forgot that he was a POW. The NVA had established a small city under the mountain that could house a battalion without cramping the men together. A small hospital was set up in one of the caverns that had a dozen wounded NVA soldiers occupying the bunks. James was impressed with the NVA ingenuity.

The NVA lieutenant hit James on the arm and pointed at one of the NVA soldiers wearing a Red Cross arm band. "You go!" James went over to the man and took the seat that was offered to him. The NVA medic dressed the scratches on James's arms and asked him in Vietnamese if he had any other injuries. James didn't understand and frowned. A North Vietnamese doctor looked up from the soldier he was sewing up and spoke in perfect English. "He wants to know if you have any other wounds that need attending to."

James looked at the doctor in shock and then answered slowly. "No . . . sir."

The doctor spoke to the medic in Vietnamese and went back to dressing the wounded NVA.

Barnett moaned. He had been dropped down near the entrance of the cave with a single guard left to watch him. The doctor looked up from his patient and spoke with rage in his voice at the lieutenant, who answered the senior officer sharply. The NVA doctor spoke one short sentence and waited. The lieutenant glared at the colonel and then obeyed. He sent two men to bring the young white prisoner over to where the doctor waited. The NVA colonel took one look at the teenager and directed his medics to make a bed ready for him. He used a scalpel to cut through the nylon cord holding Barnett, and threw the bamboo pole down on the floor. The doctor hissed the word *barbarians* under his breath, then ordered his medics to undress the boy.

Barnett lay on the cot in a semiconscious coma, drifting in and out of awareness. The doctor probed his naked body, looking for broken bones, and found three locations where he thought the young soldier was suffering from ruptures or breaks. The doctor stared at Barnett's testicles and spoke sharply to the lieutenant, who answered with a negative. The doctor looked up and glared at the lieutenant, knowing that the officer was lying to him. Someone had kicked the boy in the groin a number of times and one of the soldier's testicles looked as if it might have ruptured.

James waited until the doctor had finished with Barnett and then risked speaking to him. "Doctor, thanks for helping my friend."

The doctor looked over at the black soldier and shook his head. "I don't want your thanks. You Americans are butchering enough of my people. I am a *doctor*, and I treat *all* people . . . good and bad."

"Thanks, anyway. Doctor, do you think you could find me an interpreter?"

"Why?"

"I would like to tell the lieutenant something. . . ."

The doctor glared at the soldier. "You'll have your chance to talk tomorrow when the regiment intelligence officer will see you."

Woods lay flat on his back in the grass waiting for the helicopters to finish unloading. He needed all of the rest that he could get before climbing the mountain. Arnason sat next to him watching the Nung commandos set up the perimeter. The Chinese mercenaries worked smoothly and with little direction. They were professional warriors and had been fighting somebody or something all of their lives.

The captain took a seat next to Arnason on the matted-down grass. "The MIKE Force is going to give you their recon platoon. You won't find better fighting men in Vietnam."

Arnason nodded his head.

"They've been briefed and know what to expect. Will you be ready to leave in an hour?"

"Yes." Arnason took the shirt the Special Forces NCO handed to him. "Thanks."

"I'll be the Hatchet Force leader." The NCO spoke with authority. "We're only going as far as the ambush site to retrieve bodies. I want you to know that right off the bat."

Woods sat up. "What if some of them have been taken prisoner?"

"I know what you're thinking. I would feel the same way you do if one of my men were taken, but trust us." The sergeant looked Woods directly in the eyes. "We know what we're doing. If we try to chase them down now, they'll be waiting for us and a lot of people will get killed. We have a special team called Project Cherry that goes after POWs when things cool down."

"But they'll torture them!" Woods was letting his imagination run away.

A hurt look flashed across the NCO's face. "They might, but they've made a habit of trying to keep their POWs *alive*."

"Let's go." Woods struggled to his feet.

The Nungs moved fast through the valley and found a trail that wove its way up the mountainside. The climb was much easier even though it was about three times as long with the hairpin curves that doubled back and forth up the steep slope.

Arnason warned the Special Forces sergeant that they were nearing the ambush site, and the whole platoon changed gears and became a stealth machine. Woods constantly had to check to make sure that he wasn't alone. His mind kept going back to what he had told Spencer about not leaving him alive with the NVA; he had to make sure that his friend was dead. Woods kept trying to review what had happened in his mind. He had accepted the fact that he hadn't abandoned Spencer. The tactic was a good one, which they had used to cover for each other, and Barnett would have joined him after blasting the claymores. He thought about Sinclair and knew that it had been right to help Arnason carry the wounded man. He had done nothing wrong, he kept telling himself, he had done *nothing* wrong!

The Nung point element of three men waved for the American sergeant to go forward. Arnason accompanied the Special Forces man. They both saw the bodies at the same time. Arnason felt a cold chill traverse his spine. There were four Americans lying half undressed on the matted-down green grass. Two of the soldiers had their

heads turned away from them, but Arnason could see that
the four men were the two SF team members, Brown and
Fitzpatrick. He went over to his friend's body and looked
down at the blood.

"My God!" Arnason felt his knees shaking.

The Special Forces sergeant ordered his men to place
ponchos over the bodies until they could bring forward
some body bags. "Keep the kid back there." He spoke to
his Nung sergeant, who spoke fluent English.

"Keep who . . . where?" The words caught in Woods's
throat when he saw the bodies. "What did they do to—"
He saw the missing organ lying a couple of feet away from
Fitzpatrick. "Those bastards!"

Arnason grabbed Woods and held his hand over his
mouth. "Quiet! Keep quiet!"

Woods stopped struggling and nodded his head. Arnason
let him go, and Woods ran over and looked for Barnett. He
checked around the whole clearing and found nothing that
indicated his friend had been killed. He ran back to where
he had last seen Barnett and checked the whole area for
blood but found none. Hope sparked up inside him that
Barnett was evading the NVA and was going back to the
camp on his own.

"It looks like James and Barnett have either been taken
prisoner or they're evading the enemy." Arnason spoke
with hope in his voice.

"Prisoners, I'd say." The SF sergeant pointed at the
trimmings from a bamboo pole. "It looks like they've made
a couple of arm poles, and they do that when they've taken
POWs."

Arnason felt a pang of guilt from leaving two of his men
alive on the battlefield. He looked over at Fitzpatrick's
body. "Do you think he was alive when they . . . cut—"

The Nung interrupted. "No, he was dead. You see, there

was very little blood. If he'd been alive, there would be *much* blood!"

"Thank God. Man..." Arnason felt the tears coming. "We were together for a long time."

"Let's go." The Special Forces sergeant wanted to leave the area as fast as he could. He didn't tell Arnason, but the dead NCO was a classmate of his from the Special Forces medical school, and they had been friends for years; the dead sergeant was his oldest son's godfather.

"Woods! Let's go!" Arnason waved at him with his rifle.

Barnett woke up and opened his eyes. He saw that he was in a cave. He smelled the alcohol and medical supplies and knew that he was in some kind of medical facility. He tried raising his arm and felt the bonds. He was tied down on the bamboo cot and was naked except for the bandages covering most of his chest and sides.

"You are awake." The voice came from behind him.

The NVA colonel stepped into view. "You must refrain from cussing at field officers in the People's Army. You are very lucky they didn't shoot you."

Barnett pulled against the cords holding his arms to test their strength and felt the pain from his cut wrists.

"I must call in the regimental intelligence officer. I have been ordered to call her as soon as you woke up." The colonel spoke to one of his aides in Vietnamese.

Spencer waited quietly, using the time to check out everything within view. He was already planning an escape. The NVA intelligence officer entered the cave and spoke with the doctor for a few minutes before she approached her prisoner's cot. "I speak perfect English. I know that your name is Corporal Spencer Barnett and that you are a *hero* in the American Army for killing many of our people. I know that you have bragged to many of your fellow soldiers about the NVA you have murdered. You can be executed by the People's Army for those murders!" She took a seat on a bamboo stool next to Barnett's cot and smiled over at him. "But we are a forgiving people. Your fellow soldier, Mohammed James, has already agreed to cooperate with the People's Army of North Vietnam in their struggle to unite their country. Will you help also?"

Spencer turned his head until he was looking directly into her eyes. "Fuck you, bitch!"

"Ah!" She looked at Spencer's naked groin and smiled. "You have a very filthy tongue. I would show more respect to me if you wish to keep it, young soldier!"

Barnett tried spitting at her, but his mouth was too dry to produce anything but a small noise. She got the idea, though, of what he was trying to do.

"It is up to me what POW camp you are sent to. I can make it very easy for you and send you to a civilized camp, or I can leave you here with the field soldiers, who are very angry with Americans." She grinned. "Join us. James already has, and the two of you can live a good life and have plenty of food, clothes, and . . ." She ran her finger over his bare hip and just barely touched the edge of his pubic hair.

"*Bitch*!" Spencer struggled against his bonds. "I'd rather fuck a pig!"

She sprang to her feet. "You! You will be taught some manners . . . American!"

The survivors of the ambush and the MIKE Force had been in the A-camp for three days waiting for the weather to clear before they could be airlifted back out of the A Shau Valley.

Woods sat on the perimeter's log bunker and stared out over the fog in the direction of the mountain. He could think only about Spencer Barnett; it had become an obsession during the past three days. He still had ten months left in Vietnam, and he was going to beg the brigade commander to let him search for his friend.

"David?" Arnason had called him by his first name ever since they had returned from the patrol. "Come on, Dave, let's get packed and ready to go. The cav is sending in choppers for us and Sinclair."

Sinclair's chest had been stabilized by the Special Forces medic, who used his single sideband radio to talk with surgeons back in the Da Nang Naval Hospital. Sinclair would lose his lung, but the chances were good that he would live if they could get him back to a surgical hospital in the next couple of days.

"I'm going to say good-bye to the captain over in the command bunker, and then we'll wait by the helipad with Sinclair." Arnason paused before leaving. "Okay?"

Woods nodded his head and remained staring out over the fog. He didn't want to leave. He wanted to find Spencer.

Arnason approached the bunker and entered it from the northern door. As soon as he stepped inside, he heard a bunch of Vietnamese chattering over a radio. What caught his attention was that it wasn't a single voice but a number of people talking all at the same time. He stepped into the first CONEX container on the right after opening the steel door that was always shut when the Cav recon men were in the bunker. The captain and the MIKE Force sergeant, along with the communications NCO, were listening to one of the sensor boxes. Arnason noticed that a tape recorder was recording the whole transmission.

"What's going on?" Arnason saw the surprise on the captain's face, and then the officer held his finger to his lips and pointed for Arnason to take a seat and keep quiet. The transmission was too important for him to take the time to run Arnason out of the top-secret area.

The Vietnamese voices sounded excited, and a scraping

sound like a shovel would make could be heard. Arnason nearly fell backward off his chair when he heard James's voice coming over the receiver. *"I've carried out my part of the bargain, Lieutenant. Now you keep your promise to me."*

A soft Vietnamese voice answered someone else, and then she changed to English. *"You have proven yourself and have told me the truth, Mohammed James, and an officer in the People's Army always keeps her word."*

"You would never have found these sensors if I wouldn't have shown you where to find them."

"You said that there were six more hidden out here?" The female's voice was soft.

"Yes, but the other recon team hid them. That's all I know—that they're over there somewhere. Barnett would know if you can get him to cooperate, but I wouldn't bet on him to help."

"We'll find them, with or without Corporal Barnett. He is causing us too much trouble—" The transmission ended abruptly.

The captain looked over at Arnason. "We know now what happened to your men."

Arnason was almost in shock. "Those sensors have audio speakers in them!"

"Just two of them. The rest are vibration detectors."

"Now the damn NVA have them!" Arnason was angry. "James is a fucking traitor!"

"You're half right. James is a traitor, but the NVA don't have the devices. There are anti-tilt mechanisms in all of them that are activated when the antennas are screwed into the bases. When they dig them up, a small explosive charge burns out the inside circuits, so they have nothing but burned green boxes with fake bamboo-shoot antennas attached to them."

The sound of helicopters ended the conversation. Arnason bit his lip trying to control his anger. He looked over at the captain. "I need a copy of that tape."

"It's top-secret."

"I don't give a fuck. Send it *top-secret* to me!"

"I promise you that it'll get in the right hands." The captain shrugged his shoulders. "That's the best I can do."

"He's not going to get away with it!" Arnason stormed out of the bunker and nearly ran Lieutenant Reed down.

"Are you ready to go, Sergeant?" Reed's eyes looked extremely tired. He had aged ten years.

"Yeah!"

Barnett watched James and the NVA intelligence lieutenant return back to the POW camp. He could see that they were carrying some of the sensors, and it didn't take a great deal of smarts to know what James had done.

"*You fucking traitor!*" Barnett tried reaching through the bamboo bars of his cage.

James stopped walking with the lieutenant and turned to look at Barnett. James was wearing a new set of khaki pants with a leather belt that had a bright red star in the center of the buckle and a short-sleeved shirt. In contrast, Barnett was wearing a pair of black peasant pants, and his body was covered with insect bites and dirt.

James pointed his finger at his ex-teammate. "You had better be nice to me, honkie, or I'll ask the lieutenant to give you to *me!*"

Barnett watched James enter the bamboo-and-thatch hootch behind the lieutenant, and gave both of them the finger.

"You had better ease up a bit, young man, or you won't last very long in this camp."

Barnett looked over at the Air Force pilot in the bamboo cage across from his and slowly shook his head. "You're probably right, Colonel, but you see, I really don't give a fuck what they do to me."

"I can understand that, but you see, I have a selfish reason why you need to gut it out; if they execute you, or even if they *break* you, they'll have more time to play with *me*, and I'm afraid that there are some things that I know that could really cause some problems for the American forces. But if I had, let's say, a month . . . just an extra month . . . the things I know wouldn't be important anymore." The Air Force colonel smiled and looked over at the young soldier. "Understand?"

Spencer understood clearly what the senior Air Force officer was hinting at. He was probably one of those officers who knew a lot of top-secret stuff and was asking for some time, someone to run a little interference for him with the North Vietnamese. Barnett wasn't dumb. He knew that the NVA could make *anyone* talk about anything; it was just a matter of time and how much effort they wanted to direct at a person.

"All right, Colonel, I'll back off a little, but I want you to know that I'm not afraid of these fucking gooks!"

"Good. I'm glad that you're going to help me. What's your first name?"

"Spencer."

"Thanks, Spencer." The colonel stopped talking when he saw the guard approaching their cages. He went over to the rear side of his tiny enclosure and drank from the small cup of water he kept there. A hardwood cross was tied to the frame at the corner of his cage, and the colonel reached up and touched the very base of the hand-carved religious symbol. His thoughts were on asking forgiveness for lying to the boy. He had been a prisoner for two years, and there wasn't anything he knew that the NVA hadn't already extracted from him. He knew that if the young soldier kept tormenting the guards and officers, they would execute him to set an example for the rest of the prisoners.

Corporal Barnett sat in a Vietnamese squat, looked out at the jungle, and thought only of escape. The Air Force colonel was right: fighting the NVA would only make them break him. Escape was the answer!

Epilogue

Woods sat cross-legged on top of his fighting bunker and stared out over the rows of concertina wire at the Vietnamese laborers hoeing the new weeds sprouting up. He couldn't get his mind off Spencer. The few personal items Barnett had in the bunker had been boxed up and stored in the company supply room, but the fighting bunker brought back memories that were haunting him. He recalled the incident when he had discovered the cigar burns on Spencer, and the stories the seventeen-year-old had told him about his days in the South Carolina juvenile home. Spencer Barnett had never had a break in his life; it seemed that he was destined to lose no matter how hard he tried to pull himself up.

Woods heard voices behind him and twisted around to see who was coming out to his bunker. It was Sergeant Shaw talking to Simpson. They were laughing and teasing each other over some bar girl in Qui Nhon. Anger flashed through Woods's mind; it just wasn't fair, guys like Sinclair being badly wounded, Brown and Fitzpatrick being killed in combat, and Spencer and James taken prisoner while these bastards were getting rich selling drugs and running black-market scams. It wasn't fair!

Woods rolled over onto his stomach and extended the stock on his CAR-15. He flipped the selector switch to semiautomatic, sighted in on the sandbag wall next to Shaw, and fired. Shaw dropped down on the ground, and Woods was worried for a couple of seconds that he might have actually hit him, but Shaw started crawling for cover. Simpson hunched over and started looking around in every direction, not knowing which way to run. Woods fired three more rapid-fire rounds into the sandbags near Simpson, which convinced Simpson to run to his left. Woods smiled and felt a little better.

Sergeant Arnason heard the cracking sound of incoming small-arms fire and hurried toward the perimeter. It had sounded like an M16, but during the daylight hours there was a strict moratorium against firing weapons on the perimeter unless an NCO personally authorized it. He met Shaw, running bent over toward him, and stopped him by grabbing his arm. "What's going on?"

"Gooks! Firing at us from outside the perimeter!"

Arnason let the supply sergeant go, and hurried over to his bunker. Woods was sitting calmly on the roof watching a pair of gunships work over the area in front of his bunker.

"We receive some incoming?" Arnason's voice was skeptical.

Woods shrugged his shoulders.

"Shaw says that some *gooks* were shooting at him and Simpson."

Woods gave the sergeant a blank look and shrugged his shoulders the second time.

"It was probably a *lone* sniper harassing the base area."

"Probably." Woods took up his position against the sandbags and pulled his knees up to his chest in a modified fetal position; he was hurting, hurting bad, inside. He had to do something to help Spencer. He had to find a way to get the top brass interested in sending out a team to find the POW camp that had Barnett prisoner.

Arnason reached over and picked úp Woods's CAR-15 and touched the still warm barrel.

"It's been sitting in the sun," David said without looking at his sergeant.

Arnason turned the barrel toward his nose and sniffed in the odor of freshly burned gunpowder.

"I forgot to clean it since we came back from patrol." Woods stared at the place Spencer used to sit on the bunker's roof.

"Damn VC! Messing with our supply sergeant and battalion drug dealer like that!" Arnason replaced the weapon in the exact same spot, against the sandbag wall next to Woods. "Oh, you might be interested. I sent a telex to a Master Sergeant McDonald at the Recondo School in Nha Trang . . ."

Woods became fully alert for the first time since they had returned from the A Shau. "Why?"

"He's the best man I know of in Vietnam for prisoner snatches. That's what he was doing up at CCN—Command and Control North—when he got all shot up."

"What can he do *now*?"

"Help us to find Spencer and James. You know, David, I liked Spencer too. . . ."

Woods felt like an ass. He'd thought he was the only one who cared. "I'm sorry, Sarge."

"You don't have to apologize. Damn! If I were in your shoes, I'd probably feel the same way you do! Shit, look around you. NCOs running the black market and every one of them has an *excuse* as to why they're doing it. Officers fighting each other after a rocket attack to get their *own* award recommendations in to their buddies in personnel before the system becomes flooded. Hey, David! I've been here for *years,* boy! I've seen it all!" Arnason jabbed his finger at Woods. "Do you think for a *second* that I'd just forget about a *soldier* like Spencer Barnett?" He turned to drop down through the hole in the bunker roof. "If you *did* think that I'd forget about him, it would really piss me off!" Arnason disappeared inside the bunker. He called back to Woods. "And no more shooting at our rear-echelon types! You hear?"

"Yes, Sergeant!"

Woods opened the green metal ammo box that he used as a storage box for his letters from home and for his stationery. It was time that he wrote a letter back home to his dad and mom and let them know what was going on in the war.

Dear Mom and Dad,

I'm really rushed right now, but I wanted to thank you for the great CARE package. You can't get chocolate chip cookies over here and everyone said that they were the *best* they've ever eaten.

The weather has turned muggy, kinda like that summer we spent down in Louisiana, only it's uncomfortable *all* the time, and you always have to watch out for the bugs and stuff.

We see action pretty regularly (but I'm not going to do anything heroic mom!)

Thanks for asking about Spencer in your last letter, but I don't think he'll be able to come home with me on leave. We sort of fell out of contact, you know, those things happen.

Love you a lot,

David